TOAST

TOAST

a novel

Rex Rose

CREATIVE ARTS BOOK COMPANY
BERKELEY ◉ CALIFORNIA

For information contact:
Creative Arts Book Company
833 Bancroft Way
Berkeley, California 94710
1-800-848-7789
www.creativeartsbooks.com

The characters, places, incidents and situations
in this book are imaginary and have no relation
to any person, place or actual happening.

Library of Congress Cataloging-in-Publication Data

Rose, Rex, 1962-
  Toast: a novel / Rex Rose.
    p. cm.
  ISBN 0-88739-425-6 (alk. paper)
   1. Eccentrics and eccentricities—Fiction. 2. French Quarter (New Orleans,
La.)—Fiction. 3. New Orleans (La.)—Fiction. I. Title.

PS3618.O79 T63 2002
813'.6--dc21

                                 2002017507

Printed in the United States of America

Thanks to Mary Mitchell; Jim Bennett, Vance Bourjaily,
Moira Crone, Judy Kahn, Mark Poirier, and Mark Spitzer;
and special thanks to Andrei Codrescu, who gave me
my literary license to carry a gun.

TOAST

Introduction

THE EDITORS USED TO SEND ME OUT TO COVER THE WEIRD STORIES.
The five-thousand-dollar sex doll. The Trashcan Symphony.
Gems like that. So, naturally, when the whole spectacle
played itself out in the news, they asked me to find out about
the tattooed girl and write an in-depth piece. But when I
started to research what had actually happened, I began to see
the outline for a narrative of greater-than-magazine-format
dimensions looming in the residual smoke. I started to get to
know the people involved on an intimate level, and everything would have gone well except that, over the course of
that month, I developed kind of a little heroin habit and
missed the deadline. The editors fired me.

When I finally got my laptop out of hock, I had soured on
the idea of the article. I still felt the story of the tattoo had to
run somewhere, but I soon learned that people get touchy
when you tell their stories too accurately. Eventually, I even
had to leave town because a homicidal Cuban, whom you are
about to meet, was out to kill me, and so was the New Orleans
Police Department. But that is an entirely different story.

Some elements of this novel may seem to border on fiction, but I assure you that all of the events actually happened, at least according to the freaks who reported them to
me in an extensive series of taped interviews. You will notice
that I have included actual excerpts from the transcripts of
these interviews, which took place in the early fall of 1996

in an empty turn-of-the-century industrial building in New Orleans. I lived there on the third floor, and the interviewees upon whom I have closely based the characters would have to rattle their way up the old manually-powered freight elevator, pulling down hand over hand on a hemp rope that ran over a rusted steel pulley. Often they would bring groceries for me because I had developed an irrational distaste for leaving the building. Tall windows lined the front and back of the space, which was empty except for a bare mattress with someone else's happy memories etched all over it in overlapping stains. My visitors usually sat on the mattress, on the floor, or paced.

If you want to imagine me, just think gorgeous.

chapter 1.
TURNED AWAY

WHEN PRYTANIA RELF'S BOYFRIEND DISAPPEARED WITH THEIR
motorcycle, she packed a large duffel bag, left San Francisco,
and headed back home to New Orleans to find the tattoo
artist who had begun her snake tattoo some months before.
The trip had taken two days, and now she drove through the
night at seventy miles an hour on the raised section of Interstate 10 that crosses the swamp between Baton Rouge and
New Orleans. Close off to the right, the dark mass of a treeline blocked out a sky without stars as she slipped a White
Zombie CD into the player. Prytania, whose friends knew her
as Tania, didn't know her speakers were blown and thought
White Zombie actually sounded better broken and distorted
through her car stereo.

The Interstate rose into a long arch, sloped off to the right,
then slid down into the final stretch across the wetlands to
New Orleans, where an amber mercury-vapor glow shone
against a close overcast in the distance. As the treeline re-
ceded, a light that blazed bigger and more intensely than any
artificial light she had seen before came into view, like a sun
or a star that had deviated from its assigned trajectory to a
dangerously close orbit, or like Godzilla welding the earth to
the sky with his breath. No. Bigger and brighter than that. Had
we been there to see it, we might have felt an indefinable

sense of unease, as if Nature might take offense at the rival star. We might have seen it and said to ourselves, in that room under the one where all the talking goes on—we might have said, "Well, now we have really gone too far," but Tania had no such thoughts. She only wondered what it was, and as she looked, she began to see the details. Towering flames gushed out of a slim cigarette of a smokestack jutting from a snarl of pipes, metal armatures, tanks, and smaller smokestacks that released steam, smoke, or dim blue flames.

Her eyes began to tear, because whatever they were burning at Norco was irritating her mucous membranes. A couple of hives popped up on her wrist. She cursed and rolled up the window on the expanse of fertile, contaminated swamp that stretched out to the torched horizon just beyond which lay the Mississippi River, the intestinal tract of the country.

Every waste product between the Rockies and the Blue Ridge Parkway ultimately finds its way down the old brown sluice, be those products inanimate or otherwise, and any route you take to New Orleans, you must enter over water or swamp. By the time you get within twenty miles, they are already trying to poison you—even before you make the first bar. When you get into town, you are on a patch of land way below sea level, and once in the French Quarter, you look up over the high wall that runs parallel to the levee and see ships passing by above. Without the extensive system of earthworks and turn-of-the-century pumping stations of red brick and monstrous green piping, the water would seep in from all around and rise up into the streets, and the river— who knows what bed she would fall into?

Prytania grew up there on that alluvial island under the sea.

The car started to hesitate as soon as she came off the bridge, and by the time she made it to her old neighborhood, it was threatening to kill. She nursed it to the front of her father's house, stepped on the brake, and the engine quit running before she turned the ignition key. Prytania put on her high-heeled combat boots, then planted them on pavement dappled by a streetlight shining through the live oak branches that canopied the street. She stood up and walked to the front door, almost losing her balance from her half-asleep right leg.

The fingertips of her left hand, with their glittered purple fingernails, rested on the white doorframe, and her index finger hovered over the doorbell. Half a minute passed. On the back of her right hand rested the richly scaled tattoo of an anaconda's head releasing a red forked tongue that slipped beneath several of her silver rings and ended nearly at the cuticles of her first and second fingers. In the white light flooding down on her from the fixture above the door, at least this end of the tattoo looked complete as it disappeared under her long-sleeved undershirt. Each scale even contained a patch of white ink to make it appear to shine. Yet, from the shoulder onward, curving up and down across her back and halfway down the other arm, only the outlines of the scales were drawn in. Toward the snake's tail, the tip of which appeared from under her sleeve and rested on her left hand, even the outlines of the scales gave out. Only a pointed curving section suggested the rest of the tail. She rested the top of her forehead against the door as she studied her boots. The word *fuck* came out from under her almost waist-length curtain of purple, green, and gold dreadlocks. She pressed the glowing button.

As the reverberation of the doorbell died away, she stood up straight and heard her father inside walking heavily toward the door. Her stomach felt queasy. *Keep it light,* she told herself. *Act natural.* The door opened, and she saw her father's bulky frame stop, as if in suspended animation. Bill smelled patchouli and perspiration and saw his daughter.

Several emotions seemed to cancel one another out on his face and then left it blank. He stood there in the door in a silence broken only by bugs bouncing off of the light.

"Hi Daddy. I just broke down. I guess the Toyota only had one trip left in 'er," said Tania, trying to present a charming smile.

"Why didn't you call first?" Bill Relf had loosened the tie around his bull neck hours ago, after he came home from his law office, but he had never removed it. He was a tough customer. "You can't stay here. Your sisters. You know that. What are you doing here?"

"Jimmy fucked me over," she said.

"Tania!"

"Sorry, Daddy. I mean he turned out to be a jerk," she said, playing with one of her dreadlocks. "Dude, I was being really responsible, too, really. I swear. I got a job tending bar and got us a nice place in the Haight. It was the shit, but then he took off with the bike. I paid for half that bike, too. So, anyway, I had to get my tat finished, so I came back."

Bill picked up her right arm, as if it were a broken auto part, and estimated how much money it would take to remove the half-finished snake. He had priced tattoo removal, and now he tried to figure the number of square inches the snake covered. But he was sure it wasn't as simple as just square inches, in this case. The procedure was done with lasers tuned to the frequency of the particular ink colors. One color was expensive enough, but Bill looked at all of the fine hues and shading and realized the magnitude of the project and the incredible complication in every inch of just the snake's head. A summerhouse would be cheaper, he figured, and gave up on Tania. He still had two other daughters and knew that trying to help Tania was like throwing money in the lake. The same went for offering unsolicited advice. He dropped her hand. "They must have a half a million tattoo parlors in California. Why the hell did you have to come back here?"

"Snake's a great artist. I'm not letting anyone touch it but Snake. No fucking way. I mean no way. Sorry, Daddy."

"No. That's all right. You're on your fucking own now, and you can fucking talk any fucking way you fucking want." His temple veins bulged. Tania looked down.

"I'm sorry, Daddy."

"All right. I'll let you sleep on the couch but don't start making your phone calls till I take Missy and Camille to school, and by four o'clock tomorrow afternoon, I want you out."

"Dude, why are you being like this?" asked Prytania. "I just drove two thousand miles. It's like ten o'clock at night, and my car is fucked, okay? This is an emergency. You're treating me like shit, dude."

"I'm just sick of your bullshit, Tania. Your whole life is an emergency. Listen, just try to listen for a minute. You can't use me for a base of operations anymore. I don't want you here anymore—or your drugs, or your losers, so you are not getting another chance to live under this roof. We're agreed, then? If I let you sleep here, you'll be out by four when the kids get home?" Tania sucked on her stainless steel tongue stud to keep herself from shooting back any remarks that might keep her from getting a place to sleep.

Bill tightened his lips and shook his head.

"My God, Tania. What a piece of work. How do you expect to support yourself looking like that, anyway? You probably couldn't even make a well-paid whore, even with that body, much less marry well."

Prytania's jaw dropped open.

"You're sick."

"You're turning out just like your mother," said Bill in the violent tone that had terrified Tania as a child. But now he kept his voice down to avoid disturbing his younger daughters.

"Who's at the door, Daddy?" came a shout from upstairs.

"Nobody," yelled Bill, then turned on Tania again. "You just do whatever you feel like doing, exactly when you feel like doing it, and never consider anyone else. You're twenty-two now, and I don't know if I give a damn about you anymore, but you know what? I know I don't want to see what happens next."

"Whatever, Dad. You won't have to," said Prytania turning away. She walked back toward the Toyota to the sound of the front door closing.

Prytania had heard her father's line of logic before, but what could be wrong with doing what she wanted to do? She thought of the time she toured with Sleep, and the insane trip to Texas with Crash Worship in the back of an open truck—a big happy family with the wildest freaks on the planet lying on their backs, high as kites in the Texas sky, watching that Texas sky go by all night long at seventy miles an hour. She thought of fucking Jimmy on the roof and looking up at the moon as the San Francisco fog rolled over them. It came down to spiritual heights like these against wedding veils.

She walked toward the car thinking of Jimmy. *Fuck it. Pain's nothin'. It was worth it. I didn't want a permanent thing, anyway.* Someone always fell in love with Tania. They would see her smile, and know it would still be there when they were long gone. It was like being a part of history.

When she got to the white hatchback that she and her fifteen-year-old friend Melissa had spray-painted psychedelic, and to which they had epoxied hundreds of faceted, clear plastic beads, she looked in at the back seat. The foam rubber bulged through rips in the seat cover. She would not sleep on that tonight. She leaned against the car and looked back at the house she grew up in.

AUTHOR: What was your childhood like?

PRYTANIA RELF: It was like, you know, fucked up in some ways, and kinda normal in others. Mom left when I was really young, but Daddy was always really stable. He like always took good care of us, but you couldn't talk to him. He could be real strict, and he used to scare the shit out of me when he got mad. After Mom left, it's like I was in a coma, or something, until I was like fourteen and started like dreading my hair n' shit, but God, we had some wars over these things. [Looks up at dreads. Laughs.] I was like dead to the world, and I didn't talk much, either, until I started expressing myself with like art and clothes and my hair n' shit. It was like, you know . . .

A: Maybe you were expressing yourself that way because you couldn't communicate with your dad, or because you had turned inward after losing your mom. Maybe it was the only way you *could* express yourself.

PR: No, I was just always real creative, dude. Like, I used to have this gross, girly bedroom set that was all white with these bells painted on it, and it felt like it was just like a leash, or something. So I took my allowance and bought some spray paint and painted it all black—the bed, the dresser, the mirror frame—everything! [Laughs] Then I bought zillions of these [Laughs] these tough, big-ass nails and hammered [Laughs] fucking hammered them in all over everything. [Laughs]

A: What did your dad say?

PR: He didn't say anything. He whipped my ass! [Laughs] I deserved it, though, but I made this mobile out of like rusty chain and railroad spikes that I used to collect over there by the tracks, and I took my Barbie dolls and like impaled their crotches and stomachs on the spikes, so, like, right in the middle of my room there's this mobile with all these dead, impaled Barbie dolls just hanging there, so Daddy thinks I got molested by the priest, or something, so he sends me to this shrink who keeps trying to get me to talk about men molesting girls. It gave me the creeps. I think Daddy still blames the priest. They just couldn't understand. They thought I was nuts for wanting to look so exotic. It's not crazy.

A: You must have gone through some struggles to have your own style at that age. It is pretty extreme—your style. Why do you think it was so important to you? What made it worth getting beatings over?

PR: Well, like, the spankings weren't really that bad. You get used to it. He wasn't real extreme about punishment or anything.

A: But there must have been something behind your obsession with turning yourself into a work of art.

PR: Well, it's kind of hard to put my finger on it—[Pause] It's like when you're really stylin', that's the closest to God you're ever gonna get, you know. [Pause] It's like, when you see yourself in the mirror, it's like looking at a slide in a slide viewer, and the only way to see the light is through the picture, you know? I bet you think I'm really nuts now, too, but I don't care, 'cause, like, when I first dreaded my hair and they started to get good and I could look at myself in the mirror and toss 'em around, I'd hear electric guitars in my head, and that was like the first time I ever felt real. When people saw me on the street, I didn't feel like a ghost anymore. That's worth anything it costs. [Pause] Then I met Chucky Faggot when I was fifteen—he was twenty. He had this shaved head, and he lived down in the Quarter in this warehouse. He played electric guitar and was like full-on into Ministry. I followed him around till I finally got him to fuck me. I think he only took me home 'cause he was afraid he'd get arrested for having a minor hanging with him in public all the time.

A: Did he ever get in trouble for it?

PR: Fuck that, man. Anybody who thinks I wasn't ready for it is out of their fuckin' skull. I made him wear a rubber, anyway, so it was cool. [Pause] Chucky. Chucky Faggot. He was so cool. [Shakes head. Laughs]

(Taped conversation: 1996)

Her old nail bed would be gone now—the mobile thrown in the trash by Bill. That was okay, though. Tania smiled, and began to walk toward a chain convenience store, which sat eight blocks away.

But as she walked away from the dead car, she realized she was stuck in New Orleans with no car, no place to stay, and no money. She grinned like she had won the lottery, and something vaguely like dance came out in the way she walked. She sped up her step toward the store. There was a phone there—maybe a cab. Tania had friends. She would call Snake for a place to stay and get her tattoo finished with the same stroke. She would call Tomasso Gorbanelli and see if he could get her a job tending bar at the Green Goddess. Her way seemed clear. She had her tattoo to focus her life, and she felt her strength and youth as if they were tangible and indestructible objects.

chapter 2.
SOME DUDES

BETWEEN A PAWN AND GUN SHOP AND A HIGHLY SUSPICIOUS-looking office, which always had the curtains pulled, peeked the entrance to Snake's trailer park. He lived on Airline Highway, a four-lane, divided thoroughfare with train tracks on one side and strip malls, gas stations, evangelical churches, streetwalkers, and motels with closed-circuit X-rated television on the other. He liked to brag that he lived across the street from the hotel where evangelist Jimmy Swaggart got caught with a hooker, but he actually lived three long blocks down from there, though technically it was on the other side of the street.

Tania walked up toward Snake's trailer through the corridor created by his two muscle cars, a red '68 Challenger and an orange '71 Roadrunner. The Roadrunner had a black racing stripe, a supercharger sticking high up out of the hood, a flaming skull on the roof, and a high spoiler on the back. Snake had done quite a bit of custom work on the cars, but they still looked rough around the edges, with spots of primer making them look mangy and dangerous. Snake's pit bull–Neapolitan mastiff mix, Munchy, lunged toward Tania, stopped short only by his heavy-gauge chain tied to the trailer. Snake must have felt the trailer rock, because the door opened for Tania.

Prytania sat down on the dirty Herculon sofa, which Snake had covered with a threadbare, black satin sheet. She remembered how his small, rock-poster-covered trailer always seemed a little bigger on the inside than it looked outside. The sofa exuded the stale, garbagey odor that wafts around fundless practitioners of black magic, but the odor was mixed with the more definite smell of multiple bong-water spills probably dating back to the seventies.

Since Prytania had last seen Snake, about a year and a half before, he had turned skeletal and looked much less muscular. One of his upper teeth was visibly starting to rot. Somehow, his strawberry blond mohawk, which left two twisting snake tattoos exposed on each side of his head, seemed a little more gray and less erect than before. His longish goatee had no wave left in it, either. Even considering his advanced age of twenty-nine, he looked as if he were in very bad shape. Tania wondered *What the hell happened to Snake? He used to be so hot. I can't believe I used to blow him.* Snake closed the cabinet by the sink and returned with a bottle of Jack Daniels in his hand. He peered at her through his little round glasses.

"Yeah, you can always crash here, Tania."

"I won't take up much space. I'll make sure to keep the sofa clear in the daytime, too," she said and took a swig. "Can you start on the tat tomorrow?"

"Sure. It's about time you let me finish it."

"Really. I feel . . . incomplete, you know?"

"Yeah, really." Snake put his left arm around her, then put his right hand across on her left thigh. Very close to her ear he said, "But, Tania, you know you don't have to sleep on the couch, girl. Remember?"

"No-ho-ho, I'm off of men for a while, dude. Jimmy just fucked me over to the tune of one motorcycle. It's too fresh in my mind for me to think about anything like that right now, you know what I'm saying? It's not you," she said, sickened by his appearance, "really."

"Yeah. I understand, sweetheart. My old lady left me six months ago, and I'm still pissed off. She did a worse number on me, believe it or not. You were lucky. You don't have to worry about me bugging you for nothing. I know how you feel."

"You're so cool, dude."

"No problem . . . So, how do you want to pay for this tat, baby? You got the cash to finish it, or you want to do it in installments? It'll probably come to about eight to twelve hundred bucks, altogether."

"Pay?" said Tania with a slightly caged look, "uh . . ."

Snake had never asked her to pay him anything before. She wondered why things had changed. The anaconda was a very spiritual thing.

Tania was used to hanging around with some very overt freaks—people who could walk through a crowded mall in the middle of the Christmas season and clear a pathway fifteen feet wide. Yet she never got the knack of the whole street-wise thing. People were just people, and she'd trust them unless they screwed her over. Yet this very openness saved her from almost all real harm. They say drunk people survive car crashes because they're so relaxed when they hit.

ʘʘʘ

Big Marcus, a pensive Brit, sat amazed on a black leather sofa as he watched Tomasso Gorbanelli dance and pose while putting on a concert in his apartment in the French Quarter. Tomasso had just bought a new synthesizer with the last of the money his father had left him—a very minor fraction of the estate. The rest of the estate went to Dad's young wife in her villa on the Italian Riviera. Now the most substantial thing he had was his part ownership of a dance club called the Green Goddess. As Tomasso tapped in rhythm with wooden spoons on large, blue, glass bowls full of water, it looked as if he moved in a slightly more accelerated reality. His dirty-blond plume of a haircut jerked back and forth when he pounced from instrument to instrument, making his head look as if it were sitting on top of a spring. Tomasso often reminded people of a 1940s cartoon character—a skinny but froggish one with bug eyes and a vaguely sagging face, yet also unmistakably dashing. The breathy, reverberating chords ebbed and swelled to a repetitive beat as Tomasso threw in samples and shouted out chess moves to Big Marcus, who battled him on a Balinese chess set on an asymmetrical glass coffee table.

Big Marcus earned his name not because he was so big, though he did stand six-foot-one, but because the other Marcus that all their acquaintances knew was a dwarf—a gay, leather-clad one at that.

"I adopt the Nimso Dildo defense," said Tomasso in his rapid, clipped speech, following with a chess move.

Big Marcus, with his pale, rather puffy face oriented toward the chessboard, moved Tomasso's pawn according to his instructions. Big Marcus pulled his long, almost-black hair aside with his index finger, and the hair fell right back to its original position, twisting into slightly stringy locks. He tried unsuccessfully to concentrate on his next move through the racket Tomasso generated. A young woman with suspiciously blonde cornrows, who held the position of Tomasso's new and soon to be ex-girlfriend, sat next to Big Marcus and played with her braids. She watched Tomasso, transfixed in something closer to avarice then adoration. Her name was Judy Jane Thigpen, but Tomasso insisted everyone call her Natasha Minkski.

"Tomasso, I can't concentrate on the game with all that racket," said Big Marcus with the hint of a British accent.

"Then this will be a good exercise for you in splitting the attention," said Tomasso, "but in your case I'm not sure there's any attention to divide. You've left your flanks so badly exposed you need sunscreen. Hooplah!"

"Really, Tomasso. Give it a rest," said Big Marcus, "I know you're capable of music, but you seem to have lost the muse for the moment."

"I have to experiment if I'm going to get any new sounds."

"I know, but if I hear one more blip or bleep or bong I'll just tear my hair out. You need to create something less chaotic."

Tomasso flipped off the amps and strode over to the table, where he began to pace rapidly with his chin between thumb and forefinger.

"Make a move, Marc," said Tomasso curtly.

"You've only just moved. I need a few moments."

"You're going to bore me."

"Good. Then I'll have some company. I've been terribly bored lately."

Big Marcus translated German technical manuals for a New York firm. They would send him the German documents over the Internet, and he would send them back the English translations. He had never met any of his bosses, customers, or colleagues in person, but instead existed as a sort of point in a virtual triangle that stretched between New Orleans, New York, and Berlin. Marcus was quick at his work, though, and made a much better living than most of his acquaintances. Yet the work was tedious beyond measure. Many times he would find himself in front of his computer screen in the middle of the night, reviewing a single German word three times longer than your average sentence in English, saying, "They don't have to write like this! They do not have to write like this!" Tomasso, however, never slowed down long enough to really get bored.

"Absolutely nothing is going on," Marcus continued, coming close to a whine, "and I feel this overpowering sense of purposelessness. Sometimes I think there could be nothing worse than boredom."

"Boredom is a cliché. Your boredom is boring me. You're bored because you're boring. Why don't you make a move? Or go find yourself a girl or something?"

"It's all gotten so mechanical. Everyone around here is either seriously unstable, or you can't trust them."

"They're like that everywhere, Grasshopper," said Tomasso, not caring if Minkski might be offended. "Television has whirled their brains into a derivative paste."

"I need a beautiful, simple girl, with style and intelligence, whom I can trust not to steal my things or give me STDs. And one who's not so terribly serious. Is that too much to ask of life?" asked Marcus with a bit of theatrical irony in his tone.

"Yes," replied Marcus.

"I'm so bored."

"Let's go to the club, then."

"Oh, that should help."

"You expect too much out of life, Marc. You're just going stir crazy because there haven't been any good parties lately."

"Whatever it is, I'm unmistakably bored."

"Shut up!" snapped Tomasso. Marcus had heard that tone before, and on infrequent occasions it heralded a flurry of blows from Tomasso. Despite Tomasso's extensive liberal education, he hadn't quite broken his habit of losing his temper and periodically expressing it with his fists. Marcus had never found himself on the receiving end of one of Tomasso's blow-ups, but he didn't relish the prospect, so he took the advice and began to pretend to survey the apartment.

The ancient brick walls of Tomasso's place shone with some kind of spray-on lacquer to keep the place dust-free, and the antique plank floors held a dark, high polish as well.

Big and small pretentious art tending toward the preposterous hung on the walls—the work of friends. Huge, silk-screened fluorescent flies; little, decorated boxes; and the seven-foot-long mounted gold-leafed shark that hung above the marble mantle lent a cosmopolitan-maritime air to the crib.

When Prytania rang the doorbell, Tomasso dashed to the intercom, thinking Gator had finally arrived with the cocaine he had promised to sell him. He didn't seem happy to hear Tania's voice over the intercom but buzzed her in anyway.

"Gator must have done all the drugs before he could sell them again," said Tomasso and shook his head.

"I hardly think you need any more drugs. You're over-stimulated, as it is," replied Big Marcus. Natasha flicked an ash dismissively into an orange, glitter-laced plastic ashtray from the '50s.

Tania had gotten winded from walking up the steps and panted heavily as she entered the apartment. Marcus immediately fell in love with her—deeply in love.

AUTHOR: I understand you fell in love with Tania the first time you saw her. One doesn't hear much about that kind of thing anymore.

BIG MARCUS: Yes. It's quite embarrassing, actually. I don't know if I'm more pleased or disappointed with my capacity for that sort of thing. It does seem a rare ability for people over the age of sixteen, doesn't it?

A: So, what was it like seeing her for the first time?

M: Well, you've seen her. It was like a loud "bang" sort of thing followed by the sound of shattering mirrors.

(Taped conversation: 1996)

Tania's nose ring struck Big Marcus as a little excessive, as did her tongue stud as she stuck her tongue out to emphasize how hard the climb up the stairs had been, and he felt a sense of foreboding exhilaration. He figured she would probably make him miserable, even if he managed to get her in bed.

"Hey, dude! I missed you! How are you?" asked Tania. She threw her arms around Tomasso.

"I'm dead," said Tomasso.

"Tuh-huh. Hey, I just dropped by to see if you could get me a job tending bar at The Goddess. You still own part of it? I gotta make some money to get this tat finished."

"Isn't that tattoo one of Snake's?"

"Yeah. Isn't he great?"

"Do you . . . You might consider getting it finished in a hurry," said Tomasso as he noticed the large areas of the snake that only appeared in outline.

"I'm trying. Why?"

"I shouldn't really be telling you this but, since you have an unfinished tattoo, you should probably know that he's sick."

"Oh, my God. He didn't tell me."

"It's true, Leïbchen. You didn't let him know you in the Biblical sense, did you?"

"He's born again, too?"

"Tania, you are like a fine wine. Naïve, yet intriguing; irritating, yet voluptuous; squirrely, yet unmanageable."

"Whatever, dude," said Tania with a flagging in the strength of her voice. "Listen, who did he get it from—I mean, when did he, uh . . ."

Tomasso's voice flattened out. "He got it from shooting up with his last girlfriend—probably about six months ago. It seems like you've been gone a bit longer than that, so you couldn't have gotten it. Am I right?"

"Yeah, dude. Fuck! You had me scared for a second."

"But he just got out of the hospital a couple of weeks ago, and if he gets pneumonia again any time soon, he'll never use his needle again, and you'll be stuck for the rest of your life with a tattoo of a snake with a skin condition."

"No shit. Oh, fuck."

"Calm yourself, my little babushka. I think I can get you a job at the bar."

"Cool! Tomasso, you're the coolest."

"Flatulence will get you nowhere."

Marcus sat on the sofa and contemplated Tania's thighs, which slid around under her violet acetate pajama bottoms. Her breasts were visible in their entirety under a glued-on white sleeveless undershirt, and her high-heeled combat boots made her hips thrust forward admirably.

"Hi. What's goin' on? I'm Prytania," said Tania turning toward Big Marcus and Minkski and bobbing her head a little.

"I'm Marcus," said Marcus, looking deeply into her eyes. *Finally*, thought Big Marcus, *an uncomplicated woman with some style*.

"You guys wanna smoke a bowl?" she asked.

Natasha Minkski still continued to ignore her. She perceived Tania as a threat. Tomasso noticed, and wondered why he had brought the rube home with him. But he decided, charitably he thought, to continue seeing the young woman for a few more days, despite her lapses into un-cool, mainly because of the lack of a certain word in her vocabulary, that word being "no."

Big Marcus had often found that his old Oxford accent went over well with American women, so, even though he had been losing his accent in America, he decided to relapse for Tania's benefit.

"A very kind offer, one which I would accept were it not for a rather unpleasant side effect, called dysphoria, from which I suffer whenever I smoke mari*juana*," he said, pronouncing the second *a* laughably long. Tomasso looked at him, and raised a perplexed eyebrow.

"What's that?" said Tania with a wrinkling of her nose that Marcus found quite cute. "Is that like paranoid?"

"Dysphoria is the opposite of euphoria," said Marcus.

"Sometimes I get paranoid, too. The only thing to do when you get paranoid is go home, drink some Sleepy Time, and like get under the covers, and curl up into a ball." Big Marcus envisioned curling up into a ball with her under the covers, but realized the accent wasn't working. Tania began to pack a marijuana bud into her small agate pipe.

"We're all going to the drag show at the Green Goddess, Tania. Come along with us. It'll be great fun," said Big Marcus.

"I have a couple of things I ought to do, but I'll try to stop in later," said Tania.

Tomasso noticed that his friend seemed taken with Tania, and decided to help.

"Yeah, you better come with us," said Tomasso, "I need to introduce you around if you're going to be working there."

"Yes, do come along," said Marcus.

"Yeah, okay," said Tania, not wanting to offend the guy who had just offered her a job. Marcus felt a little queasy, but he knew that whatever pit love tossed him into could be no worse than the boredom from which he had then suffered for months—almost his whole life, really. Big Marcus had found a purpose.

Author: So you could tell he had fallen in love with her that quick?

Tomasso Gorbanelli: He was staring at her like she had a pork chop hanging around her neck. [Snickers] No, you have to understand that Marcus is really in love with himself. He just recognized some part of himself in her, and that's why he was able to project all of that. I know he'll try to give you some phenomenological argument about that, and argue the subject/object split, but really [Whispers] he likes himself. [Winks]

A: What are you talking about?

TG: [Raises his voice] You got through four years of college, and you can't follow me?

A: I forgot a lot of that stuff.

TG: OK. I'll dumb this down for you. The subject/object split: One dopey writer, that's the subject, sees the obvious, that's the object, but he can never really know the object because of his stunted mental capacity? Are you following now?

A: I think so. Is it kind of like when some obnoxious New York deejay, the subject, comes south and does too much X, the object, and starts to get Alzheimers in his late twenties?

TG: Fuck you. I'm trying to give you some insight into Marcus's personality, and you can't follow some rudimentary concepts here. Listen, Marcus loves himself, and Tania is as close to empty-headed as you can get. There's nothing upstairs, so she's like a big, white screen just waiting for some overcomplicated idiot to project the entire, jumbled content of his neurosis onto her. He looks at the screen and sees an image from the depths of his own psyche on the screen, and he thinks it's the completeness he's been looking for all along. See? He thinks he's in love with the screen but he's in love with the movie, and the movie comes from . . . [Taps his temple three times]

(Taped conversation: 1996)

AUTHOR: The way you got immediately obsessed with her seems kind of strange. Do you think you might have been projecting?

BIG MARCUS: Thank you, Tomasso. I see you've been talking with him, our local gadfly.

A: No. Why?

M: He always tells me I fell in love with Tania because of my narcissism, but it's such a simplistic argument that I can't believe he sticks to it. It's not that I argue he's wrong, per se.

I just think his argument doesn't mean anything. Nobody ever falls in love with another person. All we have are our senses, and you can count them on one hand. You take our sensory input and filter it through delusions, ideas, habits, experience, and you've already come miles from any possible direct knowledge of another person. The same things you find attractive in a new lover can end up being the things you most despise in her later. What's changed? You no longer have the glow of that immediate, striking infatuation, that's what, and she begins to disappoint the hopes *you* had for *her*. You were in love with your own reaction to her—how she fit into your hopes. You love people for the way you feel in their presence. Everybody does it. Do you understand? I'm just a striking example because I do it so damned well, and Tomasso thinks it's funny in the same way a frigid person might think the sound of someone having an orgasm is funny. But what really irritates me about his little narcissism argument is that it forces me to take my experience apart and put it back together again every time he brings it up. Tania has never disappointed my love, though I admit she has hurt me. My love for her is so profoundly meaningful to me that I just want to be left in peace with it. So, after all that rigmarole, I still love her. And that concept is even more threatening than religion to so-called rationalists like Tom. So, throw me to the lions. I will not recant. Understand? I love her.

(Taped conversation: 1996)

AUTHOR: Could you tell he had a crush on you?

PRYTANIA RELF: No, dude. I was like totally not paying any attention. Like, he was just this dude over at Tom's. He wasn't hot or anything. Looked like he needed to lay off the potatoes.

(Taped conversation: 1996)

chapter 3

THE HAND-OFF

"**W**OO-HOO," EXCLAIMED TANIA AS SHE RODE SHOTGUN ON THE wide, white seat of Big Marcus's '75 Olds Delta 88 convertible. They had just taken a spin to the Faubourg Marigny, and now returned to the Quarter. As the jasmine scent of Esplanade Avenue faded, they cruised up Decatur Street, with Spanish-style wrought-iron balconies lining the street above the first floors, with counter-culture clothing shops, restaurants, upscale bars, and downscale bars all along the street. Impeccable yuppies, gutter-punks, dissipated Goths, and obese bikers all soaked in the humid, midnight breeze in the light of ancient street lamps, neon, and shop windows. The Delta 88's eight-track tape deck played Curtis Mayfield. Both Tania and Big Marcus, who wore his vintage lime-green leisure suit and flowered polyester shirt with the wide, wide collar, felt that elusive, weightless feeling of stylin'.

Tomasso followed in the '86 Jaguar XJ6 and stared at the Delta 88, furious that Big Marcus, *his* sidekick, had outgrooved him. This could not be possible, he thought. Some electronic dance beats from CD seeped out of the Jaguars's stereo, a thin follow-up to the rich analog eight-track of Superfly. Tomasso remembered the one time he got an A-minus in psychology back in college. He had spent five times as much on the used Jaguar as Marcus had on the Delta 88 and, during the rare intervals that the Jag was in working order, Tomasso expected to be the center of attention. Tomasso had become hyper-aware that everybody on the street could see the two cars contrasted against one another unfavorably. "Fuck you," he periodically muttered like a man with Tourettes syndrome. Natasha dug around in her purse, feeling totally forgotten. As the little motorcade approached the Green Goddess, the doorman came out and removed the plastic pylons that reserved the parking in front of the club. They were a gorgeous mess. A flash from a disposable camera went off as they got out of their cars. Tomasso made for the door and entered the club quickly with Natasha, refusing to make eye contact with the peasants standing in line. Big Marcus followed with Tania. Ambient dance music saturated the dark club, which had a long bar along the right wall, a stage forward in the distance, and the deejay booth over to the left side. Masses of over-done club kids crowded the room and danced in front of the stage in the black light incrementalized by a rapid strobe light. Tomasso dashed for the deejay booth, followed by Natasha. The previous deejay immediately left the booth, and the sound of a needle scratching off a record abruptly tore the fabric of the beat. Almost all of the music at the club came off of CDs, but Tomasso kept a digital sample of the scratching needle as a trademark sound to play whenever he entered the booth so the crowd would know that he had arrived.

Marcus and Tania made it to the bar. Marcus: Crown and soda. Tania: Budweiser.

"I can't believe Snake's sick. I'm totally fucked if he dies before he finishes it," said Tania for the third time. "That would suck. I would be so dead. Hey, that guy is hot." She nodded in the direction of an excellent upper-body. "Who's that?"

Big Marcus looked. It was Gator, with Andrea standing

next to him. Gator looked like a big piece of gristle in hard angles topped with a white-blond stubble. He wore a German army undershirt with a small black eagle blazoned on it. Andrea looked less like an Andrea than anyone in the bar. Her long, straight blonde hair and blue eyes created the impression of an all-American girl, and her plaid skirt, white socks, and white shirt added a hyperbolic, girl-school touch to her look. Gator gesticulated while talking to her, and she ignored him. Looking over and spotting Big Marcus, Gator nodded to him. When he noticed that Tania stood with Marcus, he made his way over. Andrea saw him leaving, and looked over at Big Marcus. She hadn't spoken to Marcus since he had refused to sleep with her unless she got an AIDS test. He knew she had had sex, and shot drugs, with both Gator and Tomasso. Big Marcus still couldn't figure out why she was upset. Gator made his way around the bar to Marcus and Tania while flexing for Tania's benefit.

"How ya' doin', Marcus," said Gator.

"Quite well, thank you. And yourself?"

"Fuckin' great. I've got some fuckin' great coke," he said, making sure Tania could hear, "Who's your friend?"

"Oh! Pardon my manners. May I present Tania? This is Gator. He's a real Cajun." Gator was not a real Cajun.

"Cool," said an enthusiastic Tania.

"You wanna go do some coke, Tania?"

"Yeah, sure. You want to?" Tania asked, directing her question to Marcus, thereby putting Gator on the spot as if he had offered it to both of them.

"No, thank you," said Big Marcus, "I find it causes bad conversations."

"Yeah. Me too. C'mon in the back, Tania. Listen, Marcus, we'll be right back," said Gator, who had no such intention of returning her.

"Hello, Andrea," said Marcus, as he quickly moved in on her.

"Hi, Marcus," she said. She seemed bored and unconcerned.

"I've been thinking quite a bit about you, lately." Andrea only stared at him, attempting to pass for mysterious or inscrutable, but only managing vacuous. Marcus figured if he chatted up Andrea, Gator would get defensive for sure, and he would get Tania back. He didn't feel bad for leading Andrea on. To Marcus, she was a self-involved brat. "Actually, you have been appearing to me in my dreams . . ." continued Big Marcus with a straight face.

◉◉◉

Back in the dark walkway behind the stage, with the stage's backdrop curtains on one side and a brick wall on the other, Gator held out some fat lines of coke on a pocket mirror, which Tania promptly snorted. She rubbed the bridge of her nose. Her eyes widened.

"Fuck a duck!" she said. "That *is* good. Wow. Fuck a duck, dude! I never had any this good before! Shit! I can't feel my face!" she said and started laughing. He unzipped his jeans and whipped it out, hoping to get a blow job on the spot. "Dude," said Tania giggling.

"Baby, you're so hot," said Gator, pointing it at her. Tania slapped it, hard, and tried to get another couple of quick slaps in. The mirror broke on the floor.

"Fuck! Are you fucking nuts?" said Gator, trying to get it back in his pants quickly.

"Oh, sorry dude. It's dark. I thought I saw a rat. Really. Sorry," she said, still laughing. Gator got pissed and slapped her across her face, but she still didn't stop laughing.

"You like that? Huh?"

"Sometimes when I'm turned on I do," said Tania, "But dude, I am not turned on right now. Believe me. XYZ. Okay?"

"Fuck you."

The announcer's voice came over the sound system.

"Ladies and ladies," said Marilyn, a six-foot-one, two-hun-dred-seventy-five pound queen in a white sequined dress that hugged every curve, "it's time for Goddes's Goddesses. Let's hear a wonderful, warm welcome for Miss Erykah Badu!" Marilyn blew a kiss and the lights went up on a beautiful black queen, who lit candles and incense while lip-synching.

Marilyn stepped past the curtain, entered the gloom of the stage wing, and clicked toward the door to the dressing room. Little Marcus, a leather-clad dwarf, waited for her in the wing with a bouquet of flowers. Few people of any size spent as much time in the Goddess as Little Marcus, and over the last year that Marilyn had announced the drag shows, Little Marcus had begun to feel something for her—she glit-tered. She made him think of hypothetical worlds of grace and beauty beyond the bars. She was very beautiful, he thought, but there was something indefinable in her smile that drew Little Marcus in. He didn't even mind that she looked like a woman.

"Hello, Marilyn," he said in his croak of a voice.

"Why, Marcus, those are beautiful." Little Marcus couldn't believe he was doing this. If he were interested in someone, he usually was just rude and smacked him on the ass with his always-present riding crop. But something about Marilyn made him hope. He didn't even know what he hoped, but he knew it didn't have anything to do with having his sexual desire all mixed up with his desire to hurt large people. Mar-ilyn was big—very big—but she seemed to understand some-thing that many big people didn't. At least, Little Marcus fig-ured, Marilyn wouldn't laugh at him.

"I watch you announce these shows a lot, and I never seen anyone give you flowers," said Little Marcus out from under his thick mustache. His eyes were almost visible in the little slits from which they peered. "You really light this place up—a woman like you deserves to get flowers when she leaves the stage. You're a natural star." That sounded really corny, thought Marcus. Were there any decent light behind the stage, Marilyn would have looked down and seen the jaded little leather boy blush. Marilyn looked at him a little suspiciously, and smiled.

"Oh, sure, Marcus. Did somebody put you up to this? 'Cause I don't take this kind of joke very well." Marcus stiffened up.

"I brought these for you," he said thrusting the flowers out to her while looking at the hem of her gown. Marilyn's soft, powdered cheek twitched a little, and her glittered false eyelashes fluttered a few times.

"Oh. They're beautiful," said Marilyn gently. "Come into the dressing room while I put them in water. I think I have a vase in here somewhere."

👀👀

"Hey. Gator," said a cop, as Gator still struggled with his zipper in the narrow passage behind the stage with Tania still laughing at him. The zipper was stuck. Gator's frame stiffened even more than usual. "I hear you've been a bad boy," said the red-haired officer blocking the narrow passageway. Another cop stood behind him.

"Your writer bites, officer," said Gator. "Try cutting down on the TV—maybe read a book."

"Look at this, Dan," said the other cop, shining his Maglite at Gator's unzipped fly. "You got cuffs small enough for these?"

"You must be used to bigger," said Gator.

"Put your hands on your head, and turn around."

"Forgot to say 'Simon says.'" Gator went low, broke through the two cops like a fullback, and turned the corner into the crowd.

"Fuck! Cuff the bitch, and stay with her!" shouted Dan, who took off after Gator.

The cop cuffed Tania. Then Officer Dan ran right past Gator, who had hidden by wrapping himself in the stage's backdrop curtain. Dan made his way to the edge of the stage by pushing people out of his way. He stepped up onstage and surveyed the perplexed crowd for signs of Gator, unaware that Gator stood directly behind him in the curtain. Dan's badge looked like an air plug that was about to pop out of his blue-clad, steroid-inflated chest muscles, and he held his arms out from his sides in a body-builder affectation, as if his lats were too big for his arms to hang straight down. Then he flexed. He enjoyed being on the stage—looking important in his uniform. All these freaks were probably in awe of him, he thought. By this time, two new queens had taken to the stage. They were doing improvisational comedy. One of them began to impersonate a well-known daytime talk show hostess.

"I know you have a very difficult story to tell us today, but try to just let it all out," said the hostess.

"My son," said the exceedingly obese partner, "he's joined a cult."

"How did you know he joined this cult?"

"Well, they fed him steroids, made him pump iron, and he started to wear their blue uniform." She finished by conspicuously eyeing Dan, who still surveyed the crowd, which had finally begun to chuckle a little. The act had been bombing until the cop showed up on the stage, and the performers, revived by the audience response, decided to continue even if the cop fractured their skulls. The laughter and applause intoxicated them.

"Well, let's bring your son out. What do you really want to say to him?"

"I want to tell him that I miss him," the comic said in a tearful blubber at Dan, "and I'll try to be more understanding—

It's been so hard since his father left . . . and I love it hard—
Oh, son!" The queen ran up from behind Dan and began to rub
up against him like a gorilla-size Persian cat. Dan recoiled,
but she grabbed him and held on. The crowd exploded in
laughter. Dan tried to shake off his amorous new mother as
Gator stood behind the curtain only ten feet away.

He had only two routes of escape: right by Dan or across
the stage. The passage behind the stage was still occupied by
Tania and the other cop. Now, one might think that the best
choice would have been to wait until the cops gave up
looking, but the coke had given Gator too much confidence
mixed with an equal measure of impatience. He started
across the stage, looking at Officer Dan's back. The audience
began to roar as the tough-looking, industrial-type tip-toed
in his motorcycle boots across the stage, behind Dan, while
holding his black leather pants up.

To Big Marcus's surprise, Gator returned without Tania
and didn't even look upset to find him kissing Andrea's neck.

"Hey Marcus, listen. Can you hold this for a couple of minutes? I'll be right back," said Gator. He handed Big Marcus
his leather waist bag. Then he whispered, "Don't let Andrea
have it, okay?"

"Has Tania gone missing?" Marcus noticed the open front
of Gator's trousers and feared the worst.

"She's in the bathroom. Should be back in a minute."
Andrea picked up where she left off in ignoring Gator.

"Certainly," said Marcus, who had gotten very involved in
Andrea's neck. Even Tania began to seem a bit distant in his
sphere of attention.

"Good. See ya," said Gator, dashing off.

"Where were we?" asked Big Marcus of Andrea.

"You were telling me how much you like my high, white,
sheer, little school girl socks, you bad, *bad* man," said Andrea
as Marcus stroked her fluorescent-white inner thigh.

Gator made it out of the front door and almost walked into a Cuban named Jesus, who addressed him in a friendly voice.

"If you run, I'ng gonna cut choo in half, bitch," he said covering him with a Mac 10 under a coat. Gator stopped cold. The Cuban sounded like he had learned his English from rap records.

"Hey, look. I'm sorry about . . ."

"Move slow ovuh ta dat Lexus. You move too quick an I'ng gonna shoot low, 'stan what I'm sayin?"

"Yeah. Okay." Gator got into the passenger side of the Lexus, which had dark tinted windows. The Cuban got in behind him, flipped open his cell phone and hit the number for "Paulo."

"Okay, Paulo, baminos," said Jesus into the phone.

"I'm sorry about earlier, man. That was between me and Manny. I didn't intend any disrespect to you."

"So, you inten' to disrespect Manny, suckah? Manny a great man—he got style."

"Yeah, I know that. He's a great guy. It's just that, you know, we're old friends. That thing looked a lot more serious than it really was. I'm gonna pay him back next week."

"You gonna pay Manny next week? Maybe they ain't no next week fuh you, mudduhfuckuh. Doze was our drugs. Now how you gonna stick a gun in Manny's face and take our drugs widout disrespectin' me, huh, genius?"

chapter 4.
THICK

*T*ANIA RODE IN THE BACK OF THE POLICE CAR. THE RED-HAIRED COP drove, and the dark-haired cop rode in the passenger seat until officer O'Reiley dropped him off at the station. Tania wouldn't say a word, though Dan kept asking her where "that bitch Gator" had gone and saying he was going to catch him. But when the cop passed Tulane Avenue and kept driving, she started talking.

"Hey, dude, you passed the turn for Central Lockup."

"We ain't goin' there," said Dan. The caged back seat seemed to close in on Tania, her heart began to beat hard and fast, and her eyes jolted wide open.

"My father is a lawyer—William Relf—and he'll get you kicked off the force if you do anything to me."

"Shut the fuck up!" said officer Danny.

Tania couldn't think. She couldn't talk. She couldn't move, and she feared she would pee.

"What are you doing?" she asked.

"Just keep your mouth shut unless you're gonna tell me where to find that bitch Gator."

"I don't know where he is! I swear! I fucking swear to fucking God I just met him! I'd rat him in a second if I knew! Please, dude!"

"Okay, this is the last time I'm gonna tell ya. Shut the fuck up!" Dan smacked the cage with a nightstick.

He had to think. Paulo, his Cuban boss, would be angry about the Keystone Cops routine at the Goddess, and Dan figured he could blame the whole thing on his partner. Dan mentally rehearsed what he would say: *DeFilio said he had him cuffed, Paulo. He never would have gotten loose if I knew the stupid dago didn't have him cuffed. But I got the girl. She'll tell us where he is once I work on her for a while.* That sounded good enough to save his ass.

AUTHOR: What were you thinking in the car?
PRYTANIA RELF: I was thinkin', shit, I'm gonna get raped again.
(Taped conversation: 1996)

When the car passed the thick columns in front of Manny's house, turned the corner, and pulled up on the side, Dan told Tania to get out of the back seat of the squad car. They walked together through a gate in a high ivy-covered fence and rang the doorbell on the side door. Manny was short, with a slightly doughy white face and a fashionable stubble on his chin and head. He opened the door to let them in. Tania recognized Manny from around, and hoped that it would work in her favor. Once inside, Tania realized the place was an S&M dungeon. Fresh blood shone on a large X made of six-by-nines.

Oh, fuck! Oh God! She repeated silently to herself over and over again. When Manny closed the door again, they also saw that Paulo waited behind it with an Ingram trained on them.

"Dan, what the fuck are you doin', mang?" said Paulo in his black, Italian suit and greasy ponytail. Dan repeated the speech he had rehearsed. "We already got Gator, Einstein. Why'd you have to bring dat bitch here? Now we got anotha fuckin' problem," said Paulo. He nudged the gun into Tania's ribs. Paulo sounded like he had learned English from black gangsters, too.

"I'm definitely not a problem, dude. I can't see without my contacts. Seriously," said Tania squinting. Paulo grabbed her by the handcuffs, wrenched her arms up, and hung her by the handcuffs from a hook in the ceiling. She had to stay still in order to stand flat-footed on the ground.

"I gotta think," said Paulo.

"Sweetheart, just let 'em go," said Manny. "These aren't players."

"No!" said Paulo, "Let me handle my business, baby." He took officer Dan aside and spoke to him so nobody could hear. "We already found out from Gator who got da drugs. I want you to go downtown and get 'em from dis dude Marcus . . . and Dan . . . don't fuck it up dis time, or you ain't gonna have no relatives at yo funeral. Here his address," said Paulo and handed a slip of paper to Dan.

"Done, boss," said Dan and walked back toward the door.

"No, it ain't done, Dan!" Paulo shouted after him. "It'll be done when you do it!"

"Yeah, sorry, boss. I won't fuck up this time," said Dan.

"Vayase!" Dan left quickly and closed the door. Paulo looked at the door for a few seconds, then shook his head. He jerked his head toward Tania.

"Paulo, I can't stand to be around this shit. I'm going upstairs," said Manny.

"Manny, help me out, dude. Please. I didn't do nothin'. Paulo, please, I didn't . . ." began Tania.

"Who the fuck told you you could use my first name?" said Paulo. Manny continued to climb the stairs.

⊙⊙⊙

Marcus sat at home on his marbleized, dugout, pyramidal couch, which was one of Tomasso's designs. Tania must have gotten lost at Central Lockup, reasoned Marcus, because he had spent the last two hours there and on the phone with cops trying to locate her. Still Marcus couldn't find out where she had been taken. He had heard from several people that a cop escorted Tania in handcuffs out of the Goddess, just feet away from Marcus in the crowd, where Marcus had absorbed himself in Andrea's neck. Tania, he thought, must have gotten released without being booked, and it must not have occurred to her to let him know she was okay.

Gator's bag lay on the glass table top. Marcus had almost forgotten about it. He reached over, folded the flap over, looked inside, and found plastic bags full of white powder and quite a few one-gram vials full of the same. Marcus's face flushed as he realized that all the while he had questioned the cops down at the lockup about Tania's whereabouts— virtually surrounded by cops—he had had five or six ounces of cocaine on him. Marcus unzipped the pouch on the side of the bag and counted $1,235 in cash. The phone rang. It would be Gator looking for his drugs, Marcus guessed. He stared at the phone as it rang three more times until the answering machine picked up.

"Marcus, this is Manny . . . Pick up the phone, Marcus . . . Okay, listen, there's been a really huge mix-up. You've got to work with me, Marcus, or the whole thing is going to get totally out of my control. Marcus . . . Pick up the fucking phone!" The answering machine then cut him off with a beep. Marcus sat there for a moment. Something seemed terribly wrong. He took a deep breath and dialed Manny's number.

"Hello, Manny? This is Marcus. It's so nice to hear from you. I see you've left a message for me."

"Thank God you called. Look, you've got something that belongs to a friend of mine, and I need you to bring it up here right fucking now."

"What is it you're looking for?"

"I'm having a very, very stressful night, and I'm just

about to lose control of the situation, so stop with the hand-job, okay?"

"Manny, I can tell you're upset, but you're going to have to calm down and give me some clue . . ."

"You want a clue? Okay. You and your girlfriend are toast, Marcus, unless you bring it up here now, and there's nothing I can do about it. I refuse to talk about it on the phone, so I just hope you either know what I'm talking about or you're psychic, because it's getting way out of hand. This is not a test. Repeat. This is not a test, Marc."

"I'm sure I don't . . ." began Marcus, but he was stopped in mid-sentence by the sharp click. Marcus called Tomasso.

"Tomasso. I hope I'm not interrupting anything."

"Nothing much," said Tomasso, penetrating Natasha. She was holding her ankles, and her legs, which were wrapped in black spider-web stockings, stretched straight out toward the corners of the ceiling. All of the lights were on.

"Do you mind me asking what you saw of the incident at the Goddess this evening?"

"Not much, really. The cops came in and got Tania and tried to get Gator, but he got away," said Tomasso watching his cock disappear inside Minkski's closely cropped vulva.

"Have you heard from either one of them? He's not answering my calls, and no one seems to know where she is."

"No, but that cop who took Tania hangs out with Manny's Cuban boyfriends." Tomasso forgot to keep moving, and now sat on his heels.

"Well, you have certainly clarified matters a great deal . . . a great deal, indeed. I'll be over in ten minutes."

"Wait. What?"

"Someone is on the way down to get me, and I need a bit of assistance. Ten minutes."

"Okay. I guess come on over. No. Wait. Wait!" said Tomasso,

remembering Minkski. He started to move again, but she was starting to get dry. Her head lay facing sideways on the leopard skin print pillow, and her eyes were open and fixed on a hypothetical horizon of impatience. "Make it about half an hour."

"Please, Tomasso."

"Okay. Ten minutes." Tomasso hung up and tried to concentrate on Natasha again, but his cock was not as hard as before. He kneaded her breasts, stroked her legs, even tried kissing her.

"Stop," she said. He pulled out. She collected her clothing from the floor and stuffed it in her small nylon suitcase. Tomasso went to take a quick shower. He figured he might end up at Manny's at some point, and that it would be impolite to go to a gay man's house smelling like pussy.

Big Marcus hung up and went to the door with the bag, but he heard footsteps in the hall. He looked through the peephole and saw Officer Dan lumbering down the hall toward him through the fish-eye lens. Big Marcus rushed to the front of the apartment, clutching the bag, and dashed through the open floor-to-ceiling window that served as the door to the gallery. From the gallery, he threw his leg over the ornate cast iron railing and slid down one of the fluted support posts. Officer Dan kicked in the door at about the same time Big Marcus hit the street. He heard the door break in and listened from the sidewalk for a moment as Dan began to ransack his delicately balanced and eclectic decor. The squad car sat only a few feet from where Big Marcus stood. Dan had a little crucifix hanging on a chain from his rearview mirror.

👁👁👁

"I don't know what he did with it," said Tania in a matter-of-fact tone to Paulo, who held a box cutter to her breast. "Ask the stupid cop. When Gator left, *he* had it. How the fuck should I know what happened to it after that? I was busy standing around handcuffed with that other creepy pig staring at my tits. How am I supposed to know what this jerk I met two hours ago did with his stash?"

"We already beat da story outa Gator," said Paulo, "I just wanted to put a little steel on you to find out if you knew sumptin' else."

"Well, would you please cut it out now? No! Not cut! I mean could you stop now?"

Paulo pressed the button on the utility knife and retracted the blade.

"Well, where was it?" asked Tania.

"What?" asked Paulo.

"What did he do with the stash? You said Gator told you where it was."

"Bitch, what is wrong with you? Why the fuck you standin' there chained to the fuckin' ceiling askin' a fuckin' killer where his drugs is? Is you crazy, or sumptin'?"

"Sorry. I just got interested."

"Jus' shut up."

"Okay, dude."

Paulo glared at her, turned away, and walked up the stairs.

If I ever get out of this, I'm goin' straight back to Cali, thought Tania. *Well, first I'd wait until I got my tat finished. God, please get me out of this shit. If you're up there, I know I haven't been to confession since I was fifteen, but you know what I've been doing anyway. Holy Mary, Mother of God, I'm not a bad person, but I know I can do some pretty nasty shit. I wish I could tell you guys that I won't like defile myself or do drugs anymore, but I know that would be bullshit. I mean, you know me, right? What would be the use of promising? But some day I could maybe like get tired of fucking up. So why not let me live a little longer? I don't cause much trouble for anyone but myself and my Dad, I guess, but he's used to*

*it. Okay. Maybe I am a bad person, but I have faith, deep down,
even though you let my mother walk out on us. Seems like you
should owe me one for that. If you're testing me, I give. I failed.
Uncle! Okay, dude? Just get me out of this fucking shit!*

ꙩꙩꙩ

"Tomasso, be serious," said Big Marcus. "We have to get
Tania out of this."

"What do you expect me to do, get my Uzi and take out the
gay Cuban mob? And the New Orleans Police Department?"
asked Tomasso. His voice had become louder and more stac-
cato. His hands had begun to swing wider and faster as he
spoke. Big Marcus worried about Tomasso's temper. He didn't
want to mingle Tomasso's blood with his own in a meaning-
less scuffle. Marcus knew of no studies on the relative trans-
missibility of HIV through knuckle contact, so he decided to be
very sure not to mix it up with Tomasso.

"You're better friends with Manny than I am," said Marcus,
"Please come along while I return the drugs, and see if we can
straighten this thing out. I'm not asking for you to say one
word on behalf of Gator, only Tania. Please, Tomasso."

"You're making me gag. I'm not used to you getting all
ridiculous over women."

"I'm going now. Are you coming?"

"I guess I'd kick myself for missing this one."

Fifteen minutes later they sat in the Jaguar parked across
the street from Manny's restored, circa 1870 home, which sat
uptown under some mighty live oaks. Directly in front of the
house, outside of the wrought iron gate, sat Dan O'Reilly's
squad car. Big Marcus could see the crucifix hanging from
the mirror, even from across the street. He experienced a
wave of severe distaste for the officer while thinking about
the violation of his living quarters and felt a similar loathing
for Gator—the way he had abandoned Tania and left him

holding the bag. Most of all, the uneasy feeling in his gut about what had happened—was happening—to Tania radiated out to his hands and caused them to tremble.

Marcus was sitting in the passenger seat holding Gator's leather bag, which still contained the coke and cash. A plan was forming. He left the cocaine in the pouch but removed the cash, then stashed the cash under the seat.

"What did you just put under my seat, hombre?"

"Don't worry about it. There has been a slight change of plans," said Big Marcus.

"What are you talking about? You got me up here, Amigo, now you . . ."

"Please drop the Mexican theme, and take a deep breath."

"Fuck you, Amigo."

"Really, Tom. Deep breath." Tomasso turned toward the windshield, closed his eyes, and took a deep if choppy breath. "One more. Come on."

"Look, this is the calmest I am going to get speeding on methamphetamine and confronting killers! Now, what's the fucking plan?"

"I would be willing to wager that police officers never lock their car doors," said Marcus. He zipped up Gator's pouch full of coke and clutched it with whitening knuckles. "What do you say we find out?"

👀👀👀

Manny answered his door to find Tomasso and Big Marcus standing outside.

"Manny, what the hell's going on?" demanded Tomasso.

"Come in. I'll explain."

Tomasso and Big Marcus entered. As Manny closed the door, they realized that Paulo had them covered with an Ingram from where he stood exposed by the closing door.

"Put yo' hands on top o' yo' heads real slow," said Paulo.

They complied. "Manny, go downstairs and get me another pair o' handcuffs, sweetheart."

"Okay, lover, but do me a favor; don't do anything to my friends. We're just going to straighten things out, okay? Okay?"

"Just get the cuffs. I won't kill 'em . . . I can't believe we runnin' out o' handcuffs 'round here."

Manny returned half a minute later.

"Put the cuffs on 'em," said Paulo.

Manny locked their hands behind their backs.

"Sorry, Marcus. Sorry, Tom. We'll get this straightened out," said Manny.

"Now go sit on da couch. Make yourselves comfortable," said Paulo with a smirk. They complied. "Okay," said Paulo evenly, "you gonna tell me right now where the drugs is." Tomasso and Big Marcus looked at each other.

"Well, you have them. Don't you?" asked Marcus. "Didn't you send that cop who took them?"

"Don't play with me, boy. I'm just about ready to kill all four o' you. Now you tell me right now or I'm gonna start puttin' lead in yo kneecaps."

"Honestly," lied Marcus, "this big, red-haired cop broke in my door about an hour ago and took Gator's bag with the drugs in it. When he left, I went out on the balcony and saw him put the bag under the driver's seat of his squad car. We naturally thought from the confluence of events that the copper was working for you."

Paulo stood silent before the handcuffed Marcus and Tomasso for a moment. Big Marcus thought about the Spartans at Thermopylae fixing their hair before battle and wondered if Paulo greased his little ponytail especially for this type of occasion.

"Manny, go get Jesus, and tell dat punk-ass cop to stay down there an' watch Gator an' da bitch." Manny hurried downstairs, and reappeared in another half-minute with Jesus.

"Jesus, watch deez motherfuckers for a second," said Paulo, thrusting his chin in the direction of Big Marcus and Tomasso on the couch. "I got to go check out Dan's car. If Dan comes up, you tell him go back downstairs and wait."

"Si, jefe," said Jesus.

"Hey, Dan," said Paulo as he descended the stairs with Gator's bag hanging from his shoulder, "lemme see yo stick." Dan stood up and relinquished the nightstick to Paulo.

When it hit Dan upside the head, it made a pleasant, woody sort of tone—almost like a wooden wind chime. The thud as his head hit the cement floor, however, pleased the ear a bit less, but seemed just as satisfying to Paulo and Tania. Paulo straddled the unconscious Dan.

"I didn't see nothin', dude," said Tania almost in a whisper.

"Jesus!" he screamed, "todos vengan aqui!" Jesus had everybody downstairs in a matter of seconds.

"Get em all up against dat fuckin' wall!" he barked.

"What do you think you're doing?" demanded Manny

"I'm a handle my business, baby. Don't fuck wit' my business."

"Tania," shouted Big Marcus, "don't worry."

"Okay. I'll just hang here from the ceiling not worrying while they kill us!"

"I've been worried sick about you ever since you disappeared. I tried to find you at Central Lockup to bail you out, but you weren't there."

"What? What's your name again, dude?" asked Tania.

"Marcus! Marcus, for God's sake!" said Marcus, "Please don't tell me I've faced a group of homosexual Latin gangsters to rescue a woman who doesn't even remember my name."

Every viable system has a constant point that never shifts, and upon that working constant every aspect of a system calibrates itself. The system of Marcus's consciousness centered itself upon romantic love. Naturally, at crisis points, this constant exposed itself. Marcus looked deep into Tania's eyes from across the crowded room and said, "I've . . . fallen in love with you, Tania." Tania's face went blank, her jaw going slack in disbelief.

"What the fuck are you talkin' about, dude?" She started shaking her head. "You really, really don't want to do that—especially right now."

"Shut up, Marcus!" snapped Tomasso, "just stop talking . . . now!" If Tomasso were to die that day, he wanted at least to die with some cool. Tomasso's consciousness centered on the constant of cool.

"It's just that when I first saw you . . ." Big Marcus continued.

"No, dude. Just stop. Really. Just shut the fuck up," said Tania, as she noticed that their conversation seemed to irritate Paulo further.

"Yeah, shut up, your highness, the king of fuckin' England," barked Paulo.

Jesus walked in pushing a bruised, handcuffed, and bloody Gator ahead of him.

"Oh, here's the dude dat started da whole thing," said Paulo. "Take a look at him, niños. Dis' da dude dat gotcha shot."

"What?" snapped Manny. "I will not have you killing all of my friends, especially in my house. This whole thing is just not me at all. You're just going to have to find a way to handle this tastefully, or get out of my life."

"Manny, go upstairs," ordered Paulo slowly, looking Manny in the eye. Manny bristled.

"Oh! No you don't, you bitch!" said Manny. He strode up to Paulo, and gave him the flat of his hand. "Don't you ever!" he continued. "You are *not* going to tell me what to do in my house! *I* tell *you* what to do in *my* house! You can just get the *fuck* out—you and your spic friend! Get out!"

"Manny, chill out," said Paulo, putting his hand to his stinging cheek and backing up.

"Get out!" screamed Manny, pointing at the door and stamping his foot. "Get out! Get out! Get out!"

"Baby, it's okay. Okay. I ain't gonna kill yo' friends. Okay baby?"

"You think you can just go back to normal after you try to order me around in my own house? I give the orders around here, faggot."

"Okay, I know. I just get a little enojado—"

"Speak English in my country."

"Okay, Manny. I'm sorry."

"*No! No*, you are *not!* You're just afraid you're not going to get my ass anymore, and you're right!"

"Okay, baby. I do what you say."

"Okay, so this is how it's going to go! We're just going to let everybody go! Everybody walks!"

"Manny, momento. If I let the pig go, we gonna be fucked. Think. I know you don' want to hurt nobody—you a wonderful man—but some things just you gotta do. It'll be very neat and quiet. He just gonna disappear. Okay, baby? You can just go upstairs, do a few lines, and we take care of it. Okay, baby?"

Manny thought for a minute.

"This whole thing gives me the creeps," said Manny. "I don't want to know about anything, anymore. Just wait until I take our guests upstairs."

chapter 5.
CAKE

"**S**TOP YOUR INCESSANT WHINING, GATOR," SNAPPED TOMASSO from the driver's seat. Gator sat in the back seat with dry blood caked all over his face and undershirt. He was complaining a little too much about the pain, thought Marcus, considering that he wasn't really hurt that badly. He was lucky to be alive at all. Tania sat in the back seat with Gator, but refused to speak to him. Marcus sat in the passenger's seat and watched the city go by as the Jaguar sped back down to the Quarter with the top up.

"Oh, man, it hurts. Ow. I'm really hurtin.'"

"Okay. You're going to the hospital," said Tomasso.

"No, man, I don't want to go to the hospital."

"That's where you're getting out, anyway."

"No, just take me back to my place."

"Shut up!" snapped Tomasso as he made a hard left toward the monstrous 1930s brutalist edifice called Charity Hospital. Within thirty seconds, the Jaguar screeched to a stop at the doors to the emergency room.

"Here's your stop," said Tomasso.

"No, man, I'm not getting out. You said you were going to take me downtown."

Tomasso got out of the car, moved the front seat forward,

reached into the back seat, and yanked Gator out so fast that his movement almost seemed superhuman.

"Come on, Tomasso. Look. I'm not even hurt that bad," said Gator. Tomasso looked him up and down and determined that Gator was right. He wasn't hurt that badly. So Tomasso hurt him real bad. He planted the first blow just under where his ribs came together in front. At almost the same moment, he stepped on Gator's foot, clamping it to the cement, and pushed him violently backward. Gator fell. The first blow had knocked the wind out of Gator, and now he lay sprawled on his back struggling for breath. Then Tomasso kicked . . . No. The rest of this is just too ugly to describe.

The Jaguar left the crumpled Gator in a choking blast of exhaust. Big Marcus didn't say a word, because he knew Tomasso was liable to start throwing punches again, and Marcus was the closest object. The stringy little guy didn't even look like he would be able to fight. Marcus thought to himself that you really have to watch those liberals. One minute they're talking peace and justice, and the next they're beating someone outside an emergency room.

"Tomasso," said Tania, "you think I could crash at your place tonight?"

"Absolutely not," said Tomasso.

Tania almost said something, but thought better of it.

"You can stay at my apartment, Tania," said Marcus, "if you could possibly feel comfortable after my outburst earlier."

"No thanks, dude. I appreciate it, though."

"Tania, I won't be difficult. Please stay at my flat."

"You know what?" ventured Tomasso. "I'm dropping you both off at Marcus's place, and you're going to crash there, Tania. Any objections?"

"No," they said in unison.

AUTHOR: What in the world possessed you to go to Manny's house in the first place?

TOMASSO GORBANELLI: Next question.

(Taped conversation: 1996)

Tania sat on the couch as soon as she got into Marcus's flat.

"You sure know how to keep house," said Tania looking at the ransacked apartment.

"That was Officer Friendly's doing. Why don't you sleep in my bed, and I'll take the sofa?"

"I'm not getting up, dude. God, I can't believe he had me in that room like that. He could have . . . I can't understand why one human being would want to treat another human being that way. I feel so gross." Tania's voice began to waver. She held one of the couch pillows tightly, then drew her legs up and hugged them. She looked like a sleeping bird on a perch. Marcus thought he saw a glimpse of vulnerability. He wanted to go to her and hold her, but he was pretty sure that wasn't the right thing to do. He felt sure that if he did, she would break down and cry on his shoulder. That, however, never entered the realm of possibility. She hadn't cried for a long time. Not since her mother had left when she was eight.

AUTHOR: You had mentioned your mother leaving when you were a kid. How long has it been since you've seen her? If you don't want to talk about it, I'll understand. It must have hurt.

PRYTANIA RELF: Yeah, but I'm used to it by now. I saw her out in San Francisco this time. Six months ago. That's how I ended up out there the first time, too. I went to find her soon as I turned eighteen. Daddy wouldn't let me go see her, so I went to find her as soon as I could. I went by her house a few times and watched her come in and out. Followed her up the street a couple of times. I don't know why I couldn't

just go tell her who I was or give her a call first. I'd just sit
there in the car and wait for her to come out, and watch her
walk down the street, and think about . . . When she left, I
remember running after the car screaming, "Mommy! Don't
go!" [Laughs] It was like a bad movie, dude. But it made me
get more realistic. It was good for me to learn that lesson
young. I mean, life's not gonna be what you want it to be.
You're gonna be totally fucked if you wait for things to be
right. You've got to take what you can get.

A: So, you really haven't cried since you were eight?

PR: I guess. It doesn't matter. But when I went out to find
her I still had this totally stupid idea that everything would
get better when I got back together with her. I knew I was
going to go straight to her as soon as I could, and I was pissed
at Daddy for not letting me visit her. So, anyway, one of
those times I was watching her leave the house, I just got out
of the car when she was walkin' by and I was like, "Mommy,
it's me. Prytania." She was cryin' and huggin' me and we
went in and she made us tea and shit, but after I was sittin'
there with her on that couch for a while, I was, like, not wanting to be there anymore. It was funny. All that time wanting
to be with her, and then wanting to leave. It looked like she
was on like too much Xanax or Valium or something. She
had all these like Indian guru pictures and shit, and the place
was a fucking mess. Then she was trying to tell me she had
to leave us because Daddy was smothering her. What the
fuck is that? Smothering her. I mean, I used to blame Daddy
sometimes 'cause I figured he was mean to her, but, you
know, she never did shit around the house, and Daddy treated
her like a queen. She must have thought she was some kind
of southern belle, or something. So I'm sitting there on the
couch looking at my mom and thinking, *Fuck.* I thought
everything would be good again when I found her, but it
wasn't her I missed. It was me. I said I would call her again,

and left, but I didn't go see her again for about a year. It kind of fucked me up. When I came back home, I, like, felt different for my dad, but things were too far gone with us by then, anyway. I mean, I respected him more and like appreciated him for stickin' it out with us, and I even tried to be good for a while, but I'm too fucked up to keep that up for long. Yeah, that was it. It wasn't her I was lookin' for. It was me, and I knew I'd never find what I was lookin' for anymore. That little girl just blew away like a pile of leaves. I have a funeral for myself every year on the day Mommy left—June 15th, you know that?

A: Really?

PR: Yeah. It's not a sad thing. The girl I used to be might be dead, but I'll be here to remember her, and since I never grew out of her, she'll always be there to teach me to, like, stay open and happy like she was, and I'll never lose her that way.

A: What's the funeral like?

PR: It's nothing much, really. I go to the river with a bottle, and I pull out a couple of eyelashes and let 'em go over the water. Then I get drunk . . . and laid! [Laughs] Well, sometimes.

(Taped conversation: 1996)

"Let me find you a blanket," said Marcus, and walked into the bedroom.

"Thanks, dude."

When Marcus returned, he covered her with a comforter.

"Listen, dude. I don't want you to get the wrong idea, but I want you to know I really appreciate everything you did for me. I mean, I'm not saying I'm attracted to you, okay? Just thanks. All right? You're really cool."

"I still hope you'll change your mind about me," said Marcus. "You don't even know me yet."

"My mind did change, but the other part didn't. Come on, dude. I think you're really cool. I want to be your friend."

The lowest blow of all, thought Marcus. He sat on the couch next to her, and she cringed a little in anticipation of the British lunge.

"I know how ridiculous I must seem, but there is such a thing as love. You can laugh, but when it presents itself, it does so with unmistakable authority. It must be some biological thing. Pheromones, or something on that order."

"Dude. Come on."

"No. Really, I do care about you, and I have no idea why. I even did something else for you that you may find strange."

"What?"

"Gator was selling that coke he was carrying. I found twelve hundred dollars in his bag. I kept it so I could help you get your tattoo finished."

"No shit? Dude, I can't believe it. Wait. Does Gator know?"

"Certainly not. There's no reason he wouldn't think Paulo got it. But I will have you know that this is the first time I have stolen anything in my life, even though it was ill-gotten in the first place. I'm learning many new tricks."

"Dude, it's really tempting, but I can't take it, you know? I wouldn't feel right about it."

"Don't be silly. It's not like it's really my money, Tania. It's really Gator's money, and I think he owes you. Beyond that, you can consider me a patron of the arts. You'd be surprised how many works of art would never have been completed without a patron.

"You're right about Gator. Look. I'll take it to finish the tat, but I'm gonna pay you back for it, okay? This doesn't mean . . . you know. I want to get that straight."

"Of course, but I wouldn't hear of you paying it back. It seems paradoxical, but I think stealing drug money for you may have been the purest gesture I have ever made, and I don't want to part with that."

Tania sat quietly for a while peering over her knees at nothing, with Marcus watching her. Then she reached out absently and cradled a lock of Marcus's long hair in her hand.

"This would dread up good."

"How do you do that, anyway."

"It'll do it naturally if you just stop combing it, but they get all messy that way. You want to just take about this much of it and just start twisting and shit. Till it starts to knot up. You can get this special wax, too."

"I don't think so," said Marcus. Tania continued to play with his hair and he let her.

"See, it's starting to knot up already. Dude, you're so cool, but I still owe you for the money. I'll pay you like a hundred or two every month. Like, if I make a lot of tips, I'll pay you more."

"Whatever you like, but, Tania, I will ask you one favor for my trouble."

"What?" Tania asked, expecting the worst.

"Don't dude me."

chapter 6.
DOG GETS GIRL

*T*ANIA WOKE FIRST. THE SUNLIGHT CUT ACROSS THE DARKNESS OF Marcus's room in a single beam that entered through a gap left by a broken slat in the blinds. Dust swirled in the bright swath as she crossed it on her way across the oaken floor to the gallery.

In the Quarter, balconies are called galleries, and are an art form in themselves. Fluted iron pillars grow out of the sidewalks, sprout into twisting metal vines, which then form arches and railings at the second floor, grow into still more arches and railings on the third, and finally culminate in an ornate parapet of forged leaves and fronds.

Tania walked out into the light, then leaned on the deteriorating wooden handrail. She looked down a street lined with similar cages of metal foliage. The sidewalks and gutters shone wet in front of the restaurants, where black men in aprons and rubber boots hosed the sidewalks. The hiss of water coming from a nozzle merged with the rushing sound of tires on glistening asphalt as a single, late-model Lincoln Towncar rolled slowly up the street, as if the driver were hung over and fearing the slightest bump in the road. For Tania, this time of the morning always made the Quarter like an answered prayer for peace on earth, as if the city were a child who just had a good cry, and now with dirty streaked cheeks looked around startled to find the tragedy had disappeared.

Nobody was walking on the sidewalks yet. For a moment

she felt like she could forget everything, even the tattoo. She had a half-waking thought that she could maybe get up early every morning, hose down the sidewalks for a living, and be in bed by eight at night. From her left, she heard the sound of hooves on pavement. She watched the mule-drawn buggy come up Decatur. The buggy passed almost directly below her, and she heard the driver shouting a newly-invented piece of ancient New Orleans history to his load of tourists. *If the buggies are out, it's time to get going,* she thought.

Tania walked back inside and toward the bathroom for her shower. She stepped carefully over the dresser drawers, which lay askew on the floor. At that moment, officer Dan's remains were being eaten by eels and getting gnawed up by a 114-pound channel catfish in the Mississippi, but the shambles he had made of Marcus's apartment still concerned the living. Tania had to take care not to step all over the scattered computer printouts, gabardine flare slacks, polyester socks, silk pajamas, wingtip shoes, clunky-heeled Saturday Night Fever shoes, snapshots of several beautiful women and one of a parakeet holding a tiny toy gun in his beak. Flowered shirts with ridiculously large collars, a black afro-pic with a fist handle, several reference books, and an old hard-cover volume of Proust all tried to trip her or stub her black-nailed toes.

Marcus slept completely covered by a sheet on a box spring and mattress placed asymmetrically in the center of the room. When she entered the bathroom, Tania ran a bath in the old, claw-footed bathtub. She slipped in, then soaked in it while looking up at the cracking plaster and peeling paint on the ceilings fourteen feet above. The stream of hot water dribbling into the tub made a faraway sound. She lost track of time until she heard a rumbling sound through the water and her masses of submerged dreads. When she sat up, she heard Marcus knocking.

He had awakened, rolled over, rubbed his eyes, and looked

at the bathroom door with the desperate hope that she would come out of that door looking like utter hell. He would fall out of love and, consequently, out of his new nightmare. That sort of thing had happened before. When she had not made a sound in forty-five minutes, he began to worry.

"Are you all right?"

"Yeah. Just soaking."

"I thought you'd gone missing again."

"Sorry. I'll be out in a second. You got work or something?"

"No. I'm between jobs. No hurry."

Tania got out of the tub and looked at herself in the long mirror on the door—at the soaked dreadlocks losing the brightness of their color, at the rings through her nipples, nose, eyebrow, earlobes, navel, and clitoral hood, and at the poor anaconda with the featureless tail. As she surveyed herself, her shoulders sank and her head fell to one side. She pursed her lips. She looked so plain. Life always asserted its mediocrity to Tania in the mirror. The world could suck, and she could stand it. When she looked in the mirror, though, she just had to see something transcendent—had to see art. She struggled for words to articulate the way she felt, and finally said, "This half-way shit sucks."

"Yo, Marc! We got to get out to Snake's, okay?" shouted Tania.

"For you, anything."

"God," she muttered.

Within fifteen minutes they had exited the French Quarter and gotten onto Interstate 10 West, flying toward Metarie in the Delta 88 with the top up and the air conditioner on full blast. Marcus tried to engage her in conversation three times, but he only received nondescript noises in return. Tania stared off into the distance as if her eyes had become fastened on the infinity mark. Marcus realized that her place on the white bench seat of the Delta 88 was the place in the universe that lay furthest from her desires. He also began to feel dissociated as suburbia spread out around them, full of psychotic women who worship television and dangerous men with over-combed hair who drink too much beer and watch *Cops*. A few turns, and they ended up on Airline Highway.

The long car could hardly make the turn between the two little commercial buildings and into the greasy dust driveway of Snake's trailer park. Tania got out of the car and looked in between Snake's rusting Challenger and his orange Road-runner. There she saw a chained, very hot, dirty, and miserable-looking dog. Munchy rested flat on his stomach on the dust next to Snake's trailer in the glare of midday. His food and water bowls lay tipped over where he had tried to look under them.

"Munchy," said Tania in her sweetest voice, "do you want some wawa? Good boy. Good boy." Munchy just looked at her with the calm eyes of a killer.

"Aww. Good boy. Snake! Dude, we've got to talk to you. We got the money," shouted Tania toward the door of the camper, where a note written on blue-lined paper hung from a tack. "You want some wawa? Here. Let me get you some wawa, boy." Tania moved toward the faucet by the door. Munchy lunged, rocking the trailer as he reached the end of his chain. Tania jumped back.

The Romans had used Munchy's father's side of the family to fight lions and tigers in the arena, and his mother's side of the family fought angry bulls and other dogs for a living. His head looked like an anvil with skin and teeth, and his remarkably large body looked like a lumpy pile of muscle with a short tiger-striped coat. "I don't think Snake's here, dude."

"Not dude."

"Sorry. Not dude. We gotta find him."

"Shall we just call again later?"

"No. I bet that note's important."

"Tania. You're standing way too close to that murderous thing."

"He's just scared—poor thing. Snake treats him bad." He had chewed his back legs raw from the fleas. "He just needs some love."

"He needs a tranquilizer gun," said Big Marcus.

Tania turned her head toward Big Marcus and glared at him. *Mistake*, thought Big Marcus.

"How would you like to get chained out in the dust with no water and nobody to love you?"

"I think I can understand how he feels."

"Oh, yeah, you have it so bad with that fine ride and shit."

"None of that really matters."

"You could get bitches galore, dude. Why don't you wake up?"

"You've never really been in love, have you, Tania?"

"Fuck yeah, I have."

"With who?"

"Jimmy."

"What happened when he left?"

"I came back here."

"I mean, how did it affect you?"

"I don't know. I felt bad. I did."

"Did you cry when he left?"

"Aww. Munchy, Munchy. C'mon sweetness. Dude, I'm gonna go fill up this pot."

Tania walked off toward a small trailer about fifteen yards away with an old aluminum pot she had found. *Those hips!* whispered Marcus to himself as he watched her cut-off blue-jeans sway away.

"Munchy, why don't we discuss this reasonably?" asked Marcus. Munchy stared at him. "Oh. You don't? Bad luck. Perhaps you'd prefer to tear my arm from the socket instead. Oh, you would?"

Tania returned. She went to the outer radius of Munchy's chain and dipped a handful of water out of the pot with her hand.

"Oh, for God's sake, Tania! Don't even try that! He's a menace!"

"You're making me and Munchy nervous. Why don't you go stand over by your car? Go, dude!"

Marcus walked across the dusty driveway with his hands in his pockets and leaned on his car. Tania got down on her knees, dipped her hand in the pot again, and showed Munchy the shiny surface of the water in her hand. Munchy stepped forward, then back again. He finally growled. He was confused now.

"C'mon Munchy boy," she said. "Sweety pretty." The dance went on for half a minute, Marcus wincing every time Munchy got close to Tania's hand.

"Why don't you just put the bloody bowl down and let him drink? Keep your extremities away from it," shouted Marcus from across the lot.

"He's learning to trust me this way, dude. Duh. Shut up."

Munchy's huge tongue finally overfilled her hand. "Aw, good boy!" She scooped up handful after handful and delivered it to Munchy's slopping maw. "I'm gonna kick Snake's ass for leaving you chained up out here all alone. Yes, I am."

She began to stroke his jaw, and slowly between cupped handfuls worked her way to his ears and the back of his neck. When she had ladled out the last of the water, she rubbed Munchy on the back of his neck and kissed him square on the mouth. Munchy licked her face. She laughed. "Now I don't want to walk all the way over to that trailer again to fill up this pot, so I'm going to use Snake's spigot. Okay?"

She stood up, walked over to the spigot, put the pot under it, and turned on the water.

"C'mon boy!" Munchy bounded over, paws thudding on the dust. He began to lap up the water. "Good boy." Tania stepped up on the second step of the trailer and pulled out the tack that held the note in place. The note read:

to who ever gets this I am going Charity i mite be dead when you read this take care of my dog and call my sister Elizabeth Volker if I die

dont call her unless I am dead!!! (319) 372-0987 Snake

"Dude!" she hollered "Snake's sick again! He's at Charity!" Tania unhooked Munchy's chain and walked him over to where Marcus stood. The dog growled at Marcus. Munchy had dragged a two-foot long string of saliva attached to his floppy jowl all the way over to the car. At the end of the viscous string, bits of leaves and debris collected. "Munchy! Be nice," Tania admonished.

"Well, we have to go find him," said Big Marcus. The statement surprised him when it came out of his mouth.

"Okay, let's go." Tania opened the door of the Delta 88.

"What are you doing with the dog?"

"We gotta take care of him for Snake."

"Tania. Please. That's a white leather interior."

"I thought none of that mattered," said Tania. "You want to let him sit in the hot dust all day?" Marcus got stuck. "Dude, I know. You don't want to mess it up. See, this is the problem. It's not that I don't like you, dude. I'm just not a white leather interior type woman. You see that, right? Dude? You see what I mean, right? I really appreciate you helping me out and everything, but we gotta split up now, or we're going to end up wanting to kill each other."

"Tania, I don't care about the car. Put him in."

"Yeah, but now I'm gonna be thinking about the dirty dog on the white seats. We've got a basic problem. I gotta go, dude. I can catch a ride out front. I'm sure I'll see you around."

"Tania, please. I don't want you hitchhiking on Airline Highway."

"Don't worry, dude. Look at this dog. Nobody's gonna fuck with me."

"What are you going to do?"

"I'm gonna go see Snake, and see how bad it is. Maybe he'll let me stay out here. Maybe I'll crash with friends."

"Please, Tania. Don't go." Marcus failed to sound as if he was not as desperate as he felt. His voice wavered as his throat tightened up.

"Dude—Marcus—this is really nuts. You're really cool, but you kind of freak me out. I gotta go. Okay? This is going to save us both a world of trouble." Marcus stood there for a minute, and forced a nod.

"You will call?"

"Yeah, okay."

"Do you have my number?"

"No, but I can get it from Tomasso."

"If you can find him. I'm going to give it to you now, just in case." Big Marcus took a pen from the pocket of his shiny gold shirt and wrote his name and number near her knuckles across the fork of the anaconda's tongue.

"Sorry, dude. I'll see ya." Marcus's face turned stony, and he nodded. Then he watched her and the lumbering creature walk away between the two cinder block buildings that framed the driveway to the trailer park.

"Bloody dog!" said Marcus.

Before going home, Marcus stopped off at a trendy restaurant and had a Caesar salad with salmon. Then he went home, went to his bed in the center of the room, lowered himself down into it slowly, fully clothed, as if his entire body ached, and cried until he fell back to sleep. He awoke to the cricket sound of the telephone at 3:58 in the afternoon and lifted the receiver.

"Hello?"

"Dude?"

chapter 7.
CHARITY CASE

WITHIN TWENTY-FIVE MINUTES OF TANIA'S PHONE CALL, MARCUS found himself walking down the hallways of Charity Hospital. The whole place seemed vaguely yellowish with age, or maybe just misery, which had accreted since the 1930s when the grand plan of a free hospital became a reality. On his way to Snake's room, Marcus passed people with outrageous coughs, skin conditions, and genetic deformities. He thought he had grown hard to shock, but he found himself jarred by one of the creatures he saw passing by in a wheelchair and asked himself if it could have been human at all.

He found Tania sitting on Snake's bed behind a curtain at the end of a ward full of people with AIDS.

"He just got to sleep," whispered Tania. Snake lay grayish and drawn in the white sheets, his thinning Mohawk matted with dried sweat. "These nurses are the worst fucking people. They treat 'em like they're dead already."

"He doesn't look like he's in any condition to leave the hospital. Do you really think we should take him home?" asked Marcus.

"He wants to leave. He told me a little while ago that he changed his mind about the hospital, and he wants to try to finish my tat and die at home."

"What does the doctor say?"

"I haven't been able to find him the whole time I've been here. The respiratory therapist came in about two hours ago and gave him some kind of mist inhaler treatment. They got him on bronchiodialators and stuff to break the fever. Otherwise, they can't do much."

"What's the IV for?"

"Keeps him from getting dehydrated."

"I'm not sure you're right about removing him from the doctor's care, Tania. It may kill him."

"Dude, I know this sounds hardcore, but he's going to die anyway soon, and he might as well do it at home."

"His home isn't much better than this."

"Bullshit. Look around. Just wait till he wakes up, and let him tell you himself. Then you can decide if you want him to die in this shithole."

The ward remained quiet, as most of its inhabitants didn't even have the strength to cough. Marcus and Tania sat in silence for a few moments.

"Weren't you able to reach any of your friends?" Marcus asked. "Your options must have been severely limited for you to have called on me for help."

"You never find out who your friends are until you're really fucked."

"Does that mean I'm your friend now?"

"Dude, don't be . . . I just don't need . . ." Her cheek twitched in frustration. In his sleep, Snake tried to get out from under the hot sheets, muttering something about Harley Davidsons. Tania covered him again. "Look. I don't have money for a cab. I just need to get him back home in time for me to get to work tonight. It's my first night. I gotta be there. I can stay at his trailer tonight. Now you can help him or not, but I'm getting him out of here."

"You're working at the Goddess?"

"Yeah."

"Why don't you sleep at my flat again tonight? I'll drive you to check in on Snake when you wake up."

"No way, dude. Are you kidding? Look at him. I have to get out there right after I get off. I'll have money for a cab after I make a few tips."

"Of course. You're right. At least I can give you a ride out there later?"

"Yeah, okay. Thanks. You know, I hate letting you do me favors, 'cause I know you're hot for me. I wish I could just believe you want to help me as a friend."

"I think I am trying to help you as a friend."

"Oh, right."

"Well, maybe not exactly like a friend, but sometimes you really see someone. I don't exactly know what it is, but I saw you move and heard you talk—I mean, it didn't even matter what you said. It's the inflections—and I see something in your eyes that makes me feel like I know you better than if I had spent a lifetime talking to you. I see you like that all the time. Like a long-lost sister. Not really a sister, either. Don't ask me how I know how important it is that the tattoo gets finished, but somehow I can tell it's connected to more than just your skin."

"I know, dude! It's like it's . . ." said Tania, staring with wide brown eyes into Marcus's, but she never finished her thought.

"People like you and me never stay happy with regular satisfactions, do we? We always get caught up in some damned brilliant vision. I try to follow mine, but you chase yours like a wild horse. I admire that courage."

"Whoa, dude, I just got like this intense picture of this tattoo of a white horse out in a field at night raring up and chasing after this big star. Maybe I should get that next—in the middle of my back." She looked into his eyes as if seeing something she hadn't seen before, then smiled wide, and kissed him on the cheek. It nearly knocked the wind out of him. Endorphins flooded his bloodstream, and he felt a stirring in the front of his slacks.

"Tania . . . um, you know you don't really need any more tattoos."

"Hmm?"

"I mean, finish the snake, but . . ."

"Dude, but you just said . . ."

"I know. But I didn't mean . . ."

Snake woke up and said, "I need some water." Tania poured him some water from a beige plastic pitcher that sat on the high hospital table at the bedside.

"How are you feeling, baby?" Tania asked.

"I feel like total shit . . . Hey, Marcus . . . Long time no see . . . You still driving that . . . Delta 88?" asked Snake.

"I'd be happy to give you a ride in it, but are you sure you want to leave? If there were an emergency, you'd have nobody to help you at home."

"I'm going to be there," objected Tania.

"Man, I'm about ready . . . to be dead anyway. I just want to get back . . . to my own bed. Just get me out of here, Marc. Will you do that for me?" Marcus felt Snake's forehead. Hot.

"Yeah, he's going to help take you home, and I'm going to take care of you out at your place, but there's just one condition to that," said Tania, "I'm giving Munchy a bath, and he's staying inside."

"Man, he'll stink up the place."

"He only stinks 'cause you don't give him baths, jerk. I'm taking care of both of you now." Snake and Marcus both realized the futility of arguing with her. "Marcus, go get us a wheelchair."

"Are you ready to move now?" asked Marcus.

"Yeah. Get me a wheelchair. Hurry, man. Get me the

fuck . . . out of here." Within a few minutes, Marcus returned with a chair. They hoisted Snake into it, in his gown,
and headed for the elevator. A nurse with a commanding
voice stopped them from the nurse's station.

"Where you going with that man?" said the heavy-set
nurse.

"He wants to go home," said Tania.

"You can't just walk out of here with a patient. He's a
sick man."

"I just want to die at home, you fuckin' cow," said Snake.

"Snake, don't talk to her like that!" said Tania.

"Are you refusing treatment?" the nurse asked.

"Yeah."

"You already signed the admitting papers," said the nurse.
"Wait right there till I can get you a psychological evaluation
to see if you're competent to make that decision." She dialed
an extension on her phone behind the counter. "Doctor Indiri, I got a AIDS patient refusing treatment up here, but he's
got a bad fever. I need a psychological evaluation . . . Okay . . .
Okay . . . Aright . . . Yeah, I'll tell 'em." She turned to
Marcus. "The doctor says you've got to leave him here until
he can evaluate him. He'll be here in a minute."

In five minutes, a Hindi doctor in a white coat and white
turban appeared as the elevator doors opened.

"I am Doctor Indiri. What seems to be de problem?" said
the doctor.

"Our friend wants to go home," said Marcus.

"What relation are you to de man?"

"We are of no actual blood relation to him, but we're old
friends."

"Mister . . ." Doctor Indiri looked at his clipboard. "Mister
Volker. You are very seek man, and need medical attention.
Are you sure you weesh to leef?"

"Yeah, I'm sure."

"Perhaps dere is someting I can do. Why do you weesh to leef?"

"The Harleys keep pulling the covers back over me when I kick 'em off—big old panheads with no mufflers." Marcus's and Tania's eyes bugged out.

"In Mister Volker's American subculture," struggled Marcus, "panheads and Harleys refer to a woman's hands. It seems he doesn't like the way the nurses are treating him." Tania's eyes darted sideways at Marcus.

"Yeah," added Snake.

Then Dr. Indiri looked sideways at Marcus.

"Let me take your temperature." Dr. Indiri placed an electronic thermometer in Snake's mouth. "Your friend has temperature of one hundred and four degreece. Mister Volker. What ees de date?"

"I don't know. I never know that."

"Where do you leef?"

"Right across the street from the Jimmy Swaggart Happy Hooker Motel," said Snake.

"Doctor," said Marcus, "Mister Volker means—" Doctor Indiri held his palm up in Marcus's direction.

"Pleece, led me condooct my examination widout editorialization. Mister Volker, whad ees your fool name?"

"Snake—just—Snake."

"Doctor, Snake is a tattoo artist, and he only allows his nom de plume to circulate," said Marcus.

"Here ees de siduation. Your friend signed heemself into dees hospital in competent state of mind. Ad deece time heece mentally incompetent. It ees our duty to treat heem. To deescharge heem now would violate nod just de law but de confeedence he placed in us when he signed admitting papers in competent state. I'll get orderly to assist you in putting heem back into heece bed."

"Doctor Indiri," said Big Marcus, "my friend feels that his days are numbered and only wants to die in his own bed rather than here among strangers. Isn't there some way we could arrange for him to return home—perhaps with some outpatient service?"

"Perhaps I was not clear enough. It ees my determination dat heece in need of hospitalization. My hands are tied by de law. In incompetent state, heece legally incapabool of making deece deceesion to leave de care of heece physeecian. Need I clarify further?"

"What the fuck's he talkin' about, Marc? Get me outa here," said a weak but impatient Snake.

"He says you can't leave until your condition improves."

"The fuck. Listen, rag head—"

"Shut up, Snake!" hissed Marcus.

"No. No. Get the fuck out of my country, Ali Baba—you too, ya Eurotrash fruit," he continued, turning his tongue on Marcus. "You're just tryin' to get me out of the way so you can bone my girlfriend. Listen, Haj. This side of the planet is free, and I'm getting the fuck out of Dodge, you got it?"

"Dude, I am not your girlfriend," said Tania. Her hand went to her hip.

"Baby, just keep quiet."

"Yo, fuck you, motherfucker. I ain't your girlfriend or your baby, either," said Tania raising her voice.

"Tania," said Marcus, "don't get into an argument with him. He's delirious."

"Look, I don't care. He doesn't have any right to go spreading that bullshit around after all I've done for him," she yelled.

Two large orderlies showed up and Doctor Indiri instructed them to remove Tania and Marcus.

"An twenty milligrams of Valium for de patient," he shouted to the nurse. *I can't seem to get to de end of sheeft widout some terrible scene transpiring. I was so close*, lamented Doctor

Indiri to himself, *Someday dis eenternship will be over.* His shift ended in five minutes, but he would have to come back again and work all night.

Big Marcus and Tania argued outside the back door of the hospital, by the emergency room, where Munchy sat tied to a no-parking sign.

"That motherfucker still didn't have to sic those gorillas on us," said Tania. "I thought Indians were, like, more spiritual people than that." They walked toward where the Delta 88 was parked. "I've got to take a bath before work," she said, not realizing that she had taken for granted the fact that she was going back to Marcus's apartment and that the lumbering behemoth walking at their side would also be coming. Marcus said nothing. As they walked past the entrance to the staff parking lot, they saw Doctor Indiri leaving on a mid-'60s pan head Harley Davidson.

◉◉◉

Munchy lay freshly groomed and smelling of baby shampoo on Marcus's sofa as Tania got ready for work. His heavy leather collar was gone, and in its place was a thin pink ribbon. Tania wore black leather pants, belted at the waist with a wide belt from the '70s. She also wore her high-heeled black combat boots, and her threadbare, white, sleeveless T-shirt accentuated the size of her breasts. Marcus had begun to avoid looking at them because, like a hypnotist's pendulum, the horizontal sway of her chest constantly threatened to throw him into a trance. But no matter how thin the shirt, Marcus could never make out the outline of her nipples. He was beginning to think she didn't have any, and his mind stayed occupied for long periods of time imagining her without a shirt on. The other mystery about her breasts was how they could have so much horizontal push and so little vertical drag. They had obviously not been worked on, so the only explanations Marcus could think of were either sky hooks or a miracle. He found himself internally invoking the deity or his son every time she walked into the room.

She dressed all over the house. The clothes went on in the bathroom, or in the bedroom when Marcus was out of the room, then she would walk into the living room and sit next to Munchy while she applied glitter to her purple eye shadow. She would walk into the kitchen, take a swig of Wild Turkey from her chrome hip flask, and wash it down with a swig straight from a pitcher of iced tea, which Marcus had made earlier in the day. Then she'd do a deep knee bend to loosen up the fit of the leather pants and to get her used to the balance of the boots.

The decision to wear the dreads up or down took a long time. She tried it each way at least three times, walking back and forth across the floor, shaking them out, and looking at them in the full length mirror on the front door. The plum lipstick went on back at the couch, and finally she asked Marcus, who sat on the stool in the kitchen, how she looked.

"Devastating," he replied.

"It's hard work getting people to hand you dollar bills for turning bottles upside-down. You gotta put on a show."

"I would be tempted to hand you dollar bills for just breathing."

Tania laughed. "That's only 'cause it makes my tits move, dude. I gotta work. See ya 'bout two." She stuck a folded stainless-steel locking knife in her boot, and insisted on going to work alone.

After Tania left, Munchy began to stare at Marcus whenever he came in view, and growled if Marcus came within eight feet of him. He looked perfectly capable of removing a human head from a human body and spitting it back in the hole. Marcus took great care to avoid sudden motions as he straightened up his ransacked apartment. After about two hours, the apartment looked presentable again except for an eight-foot circle of debris around Munchy's throne.

After Big Marcus finished with the apartment, he went out on the gallery and sat down at his little square table with a cup of Earl Gray. *Nothing like tea*, he said to himself with the great, incomprehensible satisfaction that the English derive from the drink.

Through the elaborate wrought iron of the gallery's railing he could see the cars passing by below and the pedestrians on Decatur Street. Yet his attention focused on the conical metal light fixture from the late '50s that hung low above the table at which he sat. He had imperfectly attached a screen to the mouth of the light with beads of epoxy because he had gotten tired of watching various insects fly up into the fixture, hit the light bulb, and fall dead onto the table. He couldn't stand those yellow light bulbs, either; only white light would do. At that moment, a large, gangly mosquito tried to reach the light bulb, but bounced off the screen again and again, frustrated—probably cursing the damned screen and whatever god had put it there, he thought. An old infatuation of his, Peg, came to mind.

AUTHOR: Who's Peg?

BIG MARCUS: Peg. Peg. She was more of a what than a who. She was a generously proportioned English tart of the old fashion with buck teeth and a gummy smile. She had an easy way of going about her business that got you hooked without you knowing it. I guess I shouldn't be bringing all that up again.

A: No, that's cool. Say whatever you want. Just background, or whatever. There's still like thirty minutes left on the tape.

M: Well, I studied theology at Oxford for a time, and I . . .

A: [Laughs]

M: Yes, quite. It was all Greek to me. [Laughs] Well, the holier I tried to be, the more stock it seems the Prince of Darkness bought in me.

A: So, you're still religious?

M: That's a rather . . . No. No, I'm not. I don't see how anyone who spent so much time in Radcliffe Camera could come away from his researches a believer, but some of them do, or at least they claim to. But I read in the joint school, so I was thoroughly grounded in philosophy, as well.

A: Did you actually get a degree?

M: Oh, heavens no.

A: Why did you leave?

M: Well, actually, I found myself in a hospital bed one day, and they told me I had injured my head in the process of passing out nackered on the stone floor of a pub whilst howling for her . . . Peg. We had forged a bit of a relationship, the two of us. I guess that's what you call it when a prostitute stops charging you. She had some vision of herself as a minister's wife, or some such nonsense I suppose, but I think she was simply enamoured of having any Oxford man interested in her in a nonhorizontal position. Then some poor sod of a business student fell in love with her too, and off she went. But I know my bad judgment well enough now, and I've come to a certain peace with myself. I've determined that it's much less dangerous if I simply abandon myself to my bad judgement instead of fighting it. The strife is worse than the relationships, really, and at least I don't end up in hospital.

A: How did your family react to all this?

M: Oh, God . . . [Long pause] Well, it was a big scandal . . . [Long pause] I'm afraid I rather lost control of myself. To hell with their money. It isn't worth playing the part of the chastened reprobate. Let me think of something else to talk about.

A: Oh, come on! You can't just tell me about some big scandal and money and how you lost control and then drop the subject. Gimme a hint, at least.

M: You said I should talk about whatever I wanted.

A: Marcus, that's because you've been boring the shit out of me for an hour. Now you get to the juicy part, and you clam up!

M: Since when did this become a daytime television show?

A: It's the nature of the beast, Marcus. People are interested in this shit, not your fucking ceaseless musings on aesthetics and philosophical bullshit.

M: [Long pause]

A: Look, I'm sorry, okay? I'm still totally on edge. I just kicked, man.

M: If you're going to turn into an arsehole every time I come up here, I don't see why I should keep coming. For God's sake, I bring you groceries because you're too neurotic to go out on the streets. At least try to be civil.

A: It's not neurosis. It's called agoraphobia, and it's a new development. I've never been like this before, and I'm sure it'll go away on its own. It's just temporary.

M: If you ask me, you need to talk to someone about it.

A: I just talked to you about it. That was plenty. Now, if you don't mind, can we talk about your breakdown instead of mine?

M: All right. All right. As this is ostensibly in the name of literature, I'll go on. Where was I? Ah, yes! Scandal! I see your eyes flashing. Well, it was partly my parents' fault. They sort of just gave up on me, and they relaxed their requirements upon me to nil, though they still gave me a reasonable allowance. I had a London apartment, and no necessity to work, and I suppose I became a bit of a wastrel, you know, and I was always attracted to very radically stylish things in the first place, and this was at the height of the raves over there. All the drugs, ecstasy mostly, they caused me some problems. I was arrested, which my father fixed. Then he had to straighten out a legal situation with a girl who turned out to be fourteen years old, but really there was no way for me to know that, and I was frankly laying lots and lots of girls, until I met Serena, who I was serious enough about to propose marriage to and bring to meet my parents. She was a bit too young for me, as well, nineteen, but what really bothered my parents was that she was black . . . West Indian. They threatened to disown me if I didn't leave her, and I refused. Soon after they renounced all claim to me, the money ran out, and so did Serena.

A: [Laughs]

M: Yeah. What a shocker. [Laughs] No, she was a beautiful girl. A genuinely warm person, but, you know, girls will be girls. She just wasn't mature enough to handle my neurosis. But the point is, if I had tried to control myself and did the sensible thing about her, I would probably have spent some time in hospital or might even be dead. I just lose all control when I try to fight it. Now I'm over in America—five years now. I'm at least living a life of my own without that crushing weight of the family history and the money. I make my own living, and I don't bother with drugs anymore. Most of all, I'm no longer British.

A: Have you been in contact with...

M: No. Why should I? They'll not hear from me again.

(Taped conversation: 1996)

Marcus spent the rest of the evening sitting on the gallery just to avoid Munchy. There really wasn't much else to do in New Orleans that he enjoyed anymore. What could he do? He had rarefied tastes. The bars were full of people he couldn't stand, except for the fact that they looked interesting and stylish, which at least counted for something. But it wasn't as if he could go to a club and expect the experience to provide him with any companionship or society. The cultural life of the city stayed perpetually stultified, too, and the jazz he had always heard about in this town seemed either pretentious or hackneyed, depending on the style. Most of the other music just didn't do anything for him, either. New Orleans seemed like it had gotten in the habit of imitating itself. Perhaps the architecture saved the place for him; at least that remained genuine. But every now and then, something extremely cool happened here. Marcus spent the rest of the evening reading.

At about two o'clock, he heard Munchy start to bark, and the door opening. He walked into his bedroom through the high windows, and then into the living room. Tania knelt there cooing at Munchy, who had met her at the door. A very tall guy with a stubbly head of hair, who Marcus recognized as Sarge, stood behind her in an olive drab military jacket. His face wore an expression that seemed to combine all-business with spaced-out.

Bugger, Marcus thought.

"Hello, Tania, how was your evening?" asked Marcus.

"I did okay. This is Sarge, dude. He's going to help us get Snake out of Charity."

"I was Special Forces back in Nam. This'll be cake, man."

"It's an honor. I am well aware of your reputation. However, this operation probably won't need anyone of your particular expertise."

"Once we had to parachute into Laos to extract a CIA operative from a prison camp. This should be a similar situation. With the right team, you can get about anything done. On the way out, we cut one of the guards' heads off and stuck it on a stick out in front for a calling card. I don't mess around. Don't you worry, son. We'll secure the prisoner."

"I feel quite at ease, now, Sarge. Oh, Tania. I need to speak with you privately about a completely unrelated matter out on the balcony. Forgive my rudeness, Sarge. Would you like a drink first?"

"You don't have any codeine—morphine—something like that? The old wound is giving me trouble."

"No. Fresh out. I'm terribly sorry," said Marcus. "Tania, come along for a moment." He led her out onto the gallery. "Tania—"

"Listen, dude. I know what you're going to say, but we need someone with some experience. This is important."

"It's important to me, as well, but Sarge is—let me put it this way. What do you know about him?"

"He was a fucking Airborne Ranger in Viet Nam. That's enough for me."

"You mean he *says* he was."

"Dude, why would he lie about something like that?" Through the window, Marcus could see Sarge entering the bathroom and looking through the medicine cabinet.

"I have no idea why he chose that story. The point is, simply, that he is lying, and he was never, ever in Viet Nam, or even in the armed services at all. He's just a junky, and I think he's a little schizo to boot. Maybe he even believes his story himself, by now. I don't know."

"How do you know all this shit, dude?"

"A friend of mine who collects and sells weaponry took an interest in Sarge when he first heard his story—and Sarge is quite free with his story, I might add. At any rate, Jimmy began to talk Viet Nam–era weaponry with him, and he told me later that Sarge didn't know an M-16 from a bottle of beer. Plus, look at him. How old do you think he is? Do the math."

"Dude, I already told him he could help us out," she said. "We can't hurt his feelings now." Marcus's head tilted to the left and his eyes closed in a slight squint as if he were in pain.

"Tania, he's a junky," said Marcus. "He doesn't have any feelings."

"Maybe he does have a few problems, but he's still human—and he doesn't keep staring at my tits all the time like some people I know."

"That's because his libido has been erased by Dilaudid, my dear. Anyway, it's natural for people's attention to be drawn by moving objects. Do you know he's in there going through my medicine cabinet right now? If you're going to be staying here, you're going to have to clear your guests with me first."

"What are you going to do if I don't? Throw me out? You couldn't stand it around here without my moving objects. You're a very closed up, paranoid person, dude. He's probably just taking a leak."

"If we get him inside a hospital, he's going to go straight for the medicine cabinet, and then *we'll* be prosecuted for a drug felony when he gets caught."

"You are so fucking paranoid, dude. He's a friend of Snake's, too, and he can come along if he fucking feels like it."

Tania turned around and walked back into the apartment. She knew where she stood as she caught up with Sarge, who was just leaving the bathroom, and spoke to him. Marcus followed her in.

"Listen, I've got to get into some regular clothes," said Tania. "You guys just chill for a few minutes."

"I'm going down to get the car. It's parked in the Faubourg. By the time you're ready, I should have the car out in front," said Big Marcus. He hoped that Tania would not actually want to be alone in the apartment with Sarge without him around.

"Dude, that's a bad area," said Tania. "Sarge, why don't you go down to get the car with Marcus?"

Yes, thought Marcus.

"Can do," said Sarge.

As Sarge and Marcus walked toward the Faubourg, a neighborhood bordering the French Quarter, Sarge bored Marcus with more war stories that always ended with Sarge impaling someone's severed head on a stake. As the duo approached the B Bar, Marcus asked Sarge to go in and get a couple of drinks. Marcus handed him a twenty-dollar bill.

"I'll stand watch out here and cover the flank," said Marcus, guessing that Sarge would not realize the ridiculousness of the proposition. Marcus also bet that Sarge would walk up to everyone in the bar and offer him or her the twenty dollars for some opiates.

"Will do," said Sarge.

Sarge entered the bar, and Marcus walked away toward the car.

👀👀👀

"Where's Sarge?" asked Tania as she let Munchy into the back seat and then slid into the front seat.

"He ran into a friend who had some drugs."

"Oh, well. Fuck it."

Tania had toned down her makeup and clothing quite a bit. Now she wore jeans and a long sleeved T-shirt. She leaned back and reclined in the seat, pressing her palms into the hollows of her eyes.

"Fuck," she said. Marcus took this to mean she was tired.

"Why don't you just wait in the car while I go get him out? There's a good girl. You need some rest."

"No, I'm gonna get him out of there. Don't worry."

"Wonderful," muttered Marcus.

After parking near the emergency room entrance, they ducked and crawled past the security booth that guarded the entrance to the rest of the hospital, though the guard slept in a chair leaning against the wall inside the booth.

From there, the journey to Snake's ward didn't hold any surprises. Yet they couldn't take the regular elevator up because it opened right in front of the nurse's station. Marcus and Tania opted for the stairs. Three flights up they opened the door a crack and looked down the half-lit hallway, in the nightmarishly dim, fluorescent light toward the nurse's station. Marcus caught his breath. The strain of carrying the wheelchair they had stolen from the emergency room had winded him. He stood in the door, holding it open a bit, and kept his eye on another heavy-set nurse behind the counter about forty feet away. Marcus wondered if the place only hired fat nurses. She was a dark-skinned black woman with sculpted hair. Marcus could see her body moving a little to the music coming through the earphones of her portable radio. About thirty feet down the hall past the nurse's station stood the door to Snake's ward.

"She'll have to take a break sometime," said Marcus.

"Let's just walk down there like we own the place. I bet she'll think we belong here."

"Hi, I'm Doctor Longhair, and this is Nurse Dreadlock. We're just going to remove a dying patient in a wheelchair at three in the morning. No. I don't think that will work."

"Don't be an asshole. It's better than just sitting here."

"It's way past visiting hours. We'll be found out."

"You think she really gives a shit?"

"If she's anything like that nurse this afternoon, I should think she does."

"We can't sit here all night."

"What we need," said Marcus, "is a diversion."

chapter 8.
SARGE

SARGE WALKED INTO THE B BAR, LOOKING FOR HIS BLACK-MARKET contact. He waded through the crowd, towering over most of it, and surveyed a scene that looked like the central panel of Hieronymous Bosch's triptych of The Last Judgement, sans the return of Christ. Fantastic creatures crowded the foreground in a junkie-chic nightmare landscape, and the occasional flick of a cigarette lighter or the glow of a bizarre fixture behind the bar or at the tables recalled the middle distance of the painting where fire-gutted houses smoldered in a spreading darkness. The usual unusual clientele had crowded into the joint like the fish eating their assigned frying pans or the bagpipes playing themselves, like the curious armored demons carving up the last bit of humanity, and all waiting for something undefined and impossible to happen. Mainly, everybody just ended up getting high and having sex—usually with some implicit and denied exchange of the two. But in bars like this it got hard for the regulars to determine where drugs stopped and sex began.

Beautiful women with rich velour hats shaped like French pastries milled around or danced to the Sly Stone number coming out of the juke box—danced with guys who sported old-style tattoos of devils and eight balls and eclectic clothing mixes incorporating items from the '50s through '70s, which clashed with their sculpted, greased hair, flowing locks, or their afros and dreads in the darkness of the bar. The glass-doored beer coolers behind the bar, the juke box, and the light that hung low over the pool table were just bright enough to see by.

Sarge focused on trying to find his contact, a Vietnamese woman in a kimono. To Sarge, the place was not a Bosch painting. Everyone in the bar looked Vietnamese—was Vietnamese.

Saigon never changes, thought Sarge. *Always looks like it did back in "Full Metal Jacket." I know Saigon like the back of my hand. Everyone here knows me and whispers about me as I scan the room looking for my black market contact. The boy is strong, but he can't take much more of that pain. Damned landmines. He's only nineteen—got to get him some morphine. I have to take care of my men. Ahh.* Sarge spied a tall girl of diminutive stature, with long blonde hair and a short black bob. She was tending bar. *Bingo. I'll give her the code word.* He edged his way up to the bar and held out the twenty dollar bill Marcus had given him. He pretended to order a drink. She pretended not to recognize him. *Inscrutable Oriental.* Eventually, she pretended to come over to serve him a drink.

"What can I getcha?"

"Sunrise on the Mekong."

"Is that like a tequila sunrise?"

"No," said Sarge with a look of repressed exasperation on his face as he began to enunciate the code words very slowly and clearly. "I said *Sunrise* on the *Mekong*."

"I'll mix you one if you tell me how to make it."

"Look. I need the morphine, now! Don't try to play dumb with me. You'll end up with your head on a stake."

The young woman's eyes narrowed, she stepped back, and she walked to the other end of the bar, where she spoke into the ear of a man who resembled a heavier, oriental version of Jaws, from *Goldfinger*. Jaws, with an almost sub-sonic growl, began to lumber toward Sarge, moving hipsters to either side with his fireplug arms. He found Sarge still leaning against the bar waiting for the morphine. Jaws tapped Sarge on the shoulder. Sarge turned and looked up. *VC.*

"You have to leave now, Yankee. Fuck you, Yankee," rumbled Jaws, his steel teeth fully bared. Sarge had no choice. He had to use the ancient Oriental death blow martial art he had learned in the mist-enshrouded jungles of Southeast Asia. Sarge reached into Jaws's chest cavity and removed his heart, which still beat. Jaws looked down at his heart, unphased, and put Sarge in a headlock.

Shit! He's one of the undead zombie martial artists of the hidden jungle temple and he's applying the psychic pressure point technique. Jaws slugged him in the face.

Sarge came to on the pavement. He touched his hand to his nose and examined the blood. *Where did that come from? Where's Marcus? Must get to hospital to complete mission.* In his left hand he still clutched the twenty dollar bill. A Yellow cab sat at the corner with its roof light on. Sarge stood up, walked over, and got into the back seat.

"To the hospital. Step on it."

The Iranian Cab driver looked back at Sarge's bleeding nose and smelled his street person odor.

"You bleed on my seats?"

"Take me to the hospital, now."

"You woulden' escrew me, would you? You got no money?"

Sarge handed him the twenty dollar bill.

"Okay. I take you. If you bleed on seats, I keep whole twenny. OK?"

"Move."

"You look like a homeless. I take you Charity Hospital," said the cabby.

ⓞⓞⓞ

Sarge fit in well at Charity, and wandered around looking at the crime victims, fall victims, accident victims, and so forth, who sat in fluorescent light in the molded plastic seating of the emergency room. Sarge looked them over carefully, one by one. One of them could have been Marcus or Tania in disguise. Old women, mothers of children with earaches, and guys with hands clutched to bandaged lacerations all sat back in their seats as six-foot-five Sarge's face came within a foot of each to examine them more closely, the blood on his chin and nose vivid in the cold lighting.

chapter 9.
MORE OF SARGE'S HEAD GAMES

SARGE SAW A GURNEY ROLL INTO THE EMERGENCY ROOM CARRYING a figure wearing a motorcycle helmet. The victim's bike had wiped out at 102 miles an hour, though "wipe out" is not exactly accurate in this case. "Hit a refrigerator" is more like it. Nobody ever figured out how the Kenmore, with an automatic ice maker, ended up in the fast lane just past the apex of a small rise, but, regardless of the origin of the ice box, it was the reason the kid's head sat disconnected from his body on the gurney waiting for a doctor to pronounce him dead. A 28-year-old resident in green scrubs walked up to him, said, "You're dead," and started filling out paperwork.

"Hey, listen, man, can you do me a favor?" said a ghostly form to Sarge.

"What's your name, soldier?"

"Alfie. My friends call me Red Rover. I got kind of a problem, man."

"You look a little transparent."

"Yeah—yeah. I'm kind of dead. I'm tryin' to get somebody to take my head out of my helmet, man. It's over there on that stretcher. You think you could help me out?"

"I take care of my men."

"Thanks, man. Come on this way."

Red Rover walked back into the triage where his body

now lay covered with a sheet. "There it is. Fucking yuppie doctor didn't even look at me." Sarge pulled back the sheet. *Damned land mines.* Sarge moved his hand to close Red Rover's eyes, but Red Rover said, "No. Leave them open." Sarge tried pulling on the esophagus first, but the chin kept blocking its exit from the full-face helmet. It started to budge when he began to use the bridge of the nose and the freckled, blood-spattered cheek bones to press down upon. "You just about got it," said Red Rover. Finally it popped out.

"Jeez. Get a haircut, hippie," said Sarge as Rover's long, wavy red locks escaped their prison, "You call that a military haircut?"

Sarge looked up to ask Red Rover what he wanted him to do with his head, but he had gone. With Red Rover's head clutched by the hair, Sarge walked down the corridor to see if he could find him. Nothing. Sarge began to wander through the deserted corridors of the hospital. The swinging head started to get heavy. Luckily, Sarge came across a stainless steel IV stand, which stood about five feet high. He tied the head to the stand's cross beam with a couple of long locks and began to roll it along with him. When he came to the elevator, he had already begun to get bored with wheeling the head around. He pressed the button, and the door opened. Sarge pushed the head and its stand into the elevator and then pressed a random button that turned out to be the 3 button.

"You'll be stateside in no time, kid," said Sarge." The doors closed, leaving Sarge alone in the hall. He looked blankly at the doors and saw a MASH helicopter lifting off with Red Rover in one of its stretchers. "That kid was one of the lucky ones."

Marcus had just finished saying, "What we need is a diversion," when the elevator doors opened on the third floor. The nurse looked in the direction of the elevator, and let out a sustained scream. Marcus and Tania flinched and dove towards the wall to hide from anyone who might have been looking their way.

Red Rover's bloody face stared at the nurse from the elevator door, his eyes wild and glazed, his mouth hanging open in a silent scream. The nurse's scream trailed of into a hysterical babble of religious references. "Lawd Jesus! Help me Jesus!" And so on.

"What the fuck was that?" said Tania in a voice not much louder than a whisper. She stood closest to the door to the corridor. Marcus said nothing as his brow wrinkled. "I'm gonna take a look," said Tania. She put her hand on the stainless steel push bar of the door and started to open it just a crack, with her eye near where the door would open, but just as she did so, the door flew open. Tania let out an abbreviated yelp, and the overweight nurse plowed into her with the full force of a stampeding elephant. Tania's back hit the cement floor with such force that the thud reverberated in the stairwell. But the nurse's scrub-clad and amoebic body retained a great deal of momentum. She helplessly continued on her trajectory, landing directly on top of Tania with a subsonic shock wave like a professional wrestler administering the final body slam of a match. The nurse lifted her head, looked down on the dreadlocked face with the nose ring, and let out another shattering shriek.

Marcus with the damage control: "Good heavens, let me help you up. Are you all right? We were just leaving when we heard your scream!"

"Don't you put your hands on me! I got heads in the elevator and freaks in the stairs. You *know* they ain't payin' me enough for this shit!"

"Please, try to pull yourself together and tell me what happened," said Marcus. The nurse pulled her torso up, straddling Tania, then put the sole of her right Reebok on the cement floor. Then she pushed up on her knee with her hand.

In this way, she leveraged her bulk into a standing position. Marcus extended a hand to assist her.

"I told you not to put yo hands on me!" she said, her voice reverberating in the stairwell. Only then did Marcus realize that Tania seemed to be having a hard time catching her breath.

"Tania, are you all right?" he asked.

Tania just lay on her back with a panicked look in her eye as she tried to inhale.

"She's injured! What should we do?"

"I don' give a fuck," said the nurse. "Give the freak mouth-to-mouth or somethin'. I'm gettin' the fuck out of here!" With that she hurdled down the stairs. Marcus got down on his knees.

"Just try to relax and breathe."

Tania shot him a vicious look.

"I am trying to breathe, you retard!" she thought.

"You've just gotten the wind knocked out of you," said Marcus. She didn't even bother to shoot him a nasty look this time.

"I know I've gotten the wind knocked out of me. Shut up."

But Tania couldn't catch her breath. Her field of vision started going dark and looked like a night sky full of weird, green stars.

"Oh, God," said Marcus. He looked at her eyes fading out into a glazed look and determined he would actually try to give her mouth-to-mouth resuscitation. Marcus closed her nose between thumb and forefinger, and lowered his lips to hers. Their lips touched, and Marcus felt a little aroused, even through all of his anxiety. He blew into her mouth several times and filled her lungs with air. She really did have wonderful lips. Methodically, he continued filling her with air until she came to, choking.

"Motherfucker! Cut it out, dude! Fuck you!"

"I was just trying to give you some air so you wouldn't pass out."

"I bet you gave me some tongue while I was out, didn't you? Motherfucker. Ow. Shit. It fucking hurts."

She sat herself up with a look of surprise at the redoubling of pain.

"You must have a broken rib."

"I do not have a broken rib. Now let's fucking get Snake." She stood up, and Marcus looked at her with his mouth slightly open. She peeked out into the hall, more carefully this time, and determined that nothing stirred down the dim fluorescent passage. "Come on."

"Tania, we don't even know what drove that bison mad. There could be a maniac loose on this floor. At any rate, there are bound to be security people arriving at any minute."

She had already begun striding down the hallway. Marcus unfolded the wheelchair and followed, exasperated. Tania disappeared into Snake's ward as Marcus passed the elevator, the doors to which had closed again. When he made the entrance to the ward, Tania already sat on the edge of Snake's bed. Apparently he could breathe enough to forego the oxygen mask, but the tank sat next to his bed. As Marcus approached, he began to hear him talking, taking short, shallow breaths between every second or third word.

" . . .the hell . . .outa here . . .these nurses are . . .sadistic . . .Fuck . . .I'm so weak . . .help me up . . ."

"Are you sure you can move?" asked Marcus.

"Bring that chair . . .around."

Marcus brought the chair, sat down on the bed, and lifted Snake up into a sitting position by grabbing him under his wet armpits.

"Wait . . .wait," said Snake, who seemed about to lose consciousness.

"If we're going to do this, we gotta hurry," said Tania.

"Yeah . . .yeah . . .okay . . .," said Snake. He slowly hung his legs off the edge of the bed, and Tania and Marcus got on either side and lifted.

AUTHOR: Oh, come on. I can't believe this shit.

PRYTANIA RELF: What, dude?

A: I mean, the whole idea was totally nuts to start with, and then it was obviously blowing up in your face. Why didn't you just get the hell out of there?

PR: I don't get why everyone says it was so fucking crazy. You weren't the one with an unfinished tattoo covering like half your body, dude. I was totally desperate. I had to get him out, and he was begging me to get him out, too. My whole life I got people telling me, "You can't do this. You can't do that," and then guess what. I do it anyway. And who are you to be telling me I'm crazy? Dude. You're so scared to leave the fucking building you have to get me to shop for you. Remember?

A: This is just a temporary thing.

PR: So was trying to sneak Snake out of the hospital, dude.

Tania and Marcus managed to get Snake into the chair without much trouble. Tania lifted the oxygen tank, and put it on his lap, also throwing a bag of saline solution on top.

"Let's get the fuck," said Tania feverishly, now feeling the flush of theft on her face. They raced down the hallway and pressed the elevator down button. Tania tapped her foot nervously and pressed the button over and over again even though it already glowed yellow. Marcus stood and watched the numbers.

Then a loud voice shattered the quiet.

"You stop! Get away from de elevator!"

The wavy cadence identified the voice as that of Doctor

Indiri, even before Marcus and Tania turned around to face him. "I told you earlier that he cannot leaf! Heece life ees een danger!" Doctor Indiri stood behind the nurses' station with the phone in his hand. "Security to de tird floor. Come queekly!"

"Doctor," began Marcus, "please call off the dogs. We're not criminals. We simply wish to give this man his deathbed wish, to die at home."

"I have explained dees to you earlier!" exclaimed Doctor Indiri, his voice quavering, "Now you have crossed de line into kidnapping!"

"Dude, Snake is not a kid and he can decide for himself."

"I beg of you, Doctor, please. I appeal to you as a Hindu. The way these Americans die is unnatural. You must see that. Think back on how your people deal with the dying, and ask yourself if you want to condemn this man to such a death as you have laid before him."

"Dees man is not dead yet, and cood be saved. As to my peepool, dey often die in de open and lie where dey fall for days out in the streets wid de rats and de flies. Dere is in fact no healthcare seestem to speak of for many many of my peepool, and how dare you, an Eenglishman, presume to give me a lesson on humanity! Deece is out of my hands now. De police will decide what to do."

"Turn me around," said Snake, still facing the elevator doors.

"Shut up, Snake!" said Marcus and Tania in unison. They continued to try to soften Doctor Indiri's will, and argued their points so intently, in fact, that they didn't notice when the elevator doors opened.

"One of your . . .other patients, Doc?" said Snake as loudly as he could manage.

They all turned to look at Rover's silently screaming face. Tania's scream, however, was not silent. Her knees bent, and she almost doubled over from exertion of the athletic shriek. She took a couple of hunched-over steps backward as if the air blast had propelled her like a rocket.

"My *God!*" shouted Marcus, but his mind cleared instantly when the idea hit him. "Is this your idea of a joke? Well, this is not funny, doctor! Look at her!" Tania cried and hung on to Marcus. "This little game of yours could have psychologically disastrous consequences for her. You and your sick staff may think it's fun to play with cadavers on the night shift, but normal people who sit on juries have not been desensitized to this kind of ghoulish behavior. This hospital is going to pay dearly for any damages this causes. I guarantee you that!" said Marcus, and then threw in a derisive laugh before he finished with the sardonically enunciated "Doctor."

"I assure you I don't know nothing about dees ting! I never see such a ting as long as I am here!"

"I'll see you in court! I promise you that!"

"No! No, you musn't file a . . . De image of dees ospital ees bad enough. Do you wan't our funding cut again? We can barely afford to take care of men like . . . like . . .."

"Snake," said Snake.

"Yes. Like Snake here," finished Doctor Indiri.

"I can see the kind of care you give, and I am going to do my best to shut this place down and see to it that you never practice."

"Look! I let you go! I do not say nothing!" Doctor Indiri rushed from behind the nurse's station and held the door of the elevator open just as it began to close again. He pulled the head and the IV stand out of the elevator. "Come! Get een. You may go freely."

"No. We'll wait till the police arrive." Tania still cried hysterically on Marcus's shoulder. "Look what you've done to her."

"What about Snake? Heece going to end up staying heer if you don't take heem now!"

Marcus paused for a moment.

"I suppose you're right about that. All right. We'll go, but I hope you meditate on the inhumanity of your nightly pastimes, Doctor. Push him into the elevator." Doctor Indiri pushed Snake's wheelchair into the elevator, and Marcus followed, pulling Tania with him. He pushed the "1" button. Doctor Indiri stepped out of the elevator and turned to watch them disappear, wringing his hands. Snake lifted his chin from his chest, looked up at Doctor Indiri's turban, and began to hum a snake charmer's song as the doors closed. Tania, now standing on her own but still breathing heavily and crying, said, "What the fuck was that? That was some fucked up shit there, dude! I mean, dude, that was so fucking fucked up. Oh, shit, there's blood on the floor!" She dove back into Marcus's arms.

"I know," said Marcus. "Just don't look down."

"Dude. Really. Is this shit, like, really happening?"

"I think so."

When the doors opened again, the first thing they saw was Sarge pushing the elevator button.

"How was the ride? Catch any flak?" asked Sarge.

"How did you...?" asked Marcus.

"Just trying to get some news, soldier. Did you see a long-haired kid back at the medical unit—a red head? With a neck wound?"

"*Oh!* Maybe so. We thought a high spirited intern might have sent him up."

"No. I put him on the chopper personally. I can't let my men down. Snake. Long time no see. Sorry about your legs. Damned landmines. You'll be out of this camp in no time."

"Quite," said Marcus. "Let's go. Now."

"I can't leave without finding out what happened to that kid," said Sarge.

"He's dead, Sarge. You have to let it go," said Marcus.

"No. He couldn't have. His wounds weren't that bad."

"It was poison shrapnel," said Big Marcus. Sarge looked confused. "Don't worry," said Big Marcus. "We gave him a proper burial at Arlington. His name is on the Vietnam War Memorial with flowers beneath it." Sarge began to choke up.

"When we came back they spat on us—called us baby killers. Thank you. At least a few Americans like you still care."

"Not at all," said Marcus. "Now let's get this POW to safety, shall we?"

"Right. I guess I got a little emotional. You can get close to cracking up out here sometimes. I'll take point. You take care of the woman and Snake, but don't lag behind. I'm counting on you, soldier."

"Yes, sir," said Marcus. Sarge hacked back the dense foliage in the tropical darkness, clearing the way for their escape.

chapter 10.
TRAILER TROUBLE

SNAKE LAY AT HOME IN HIS BED, SHIVERING. TANIA HAD TOLD Marcus to get lost, hours ago. She sat on the couch with the phone receiver held up to her ear talking to Aunt Mazzie, the witch, with Munchy at her feet.

"Yeah . . . Can you help us out? . . . No . . . Huh-unh . . . Nope . . . Well I guess so, hold on." She put her hand over the receiver. "Hey Snake! Snake, dude, wake up. She needs like three hundred bucks."

"Fuck her . . . I don't believe . . . in that shit."

"Dude, this is no time to get cheap. You got to do it. I'm gonna be payin' you, man. You can afford it."

"Will you shut the fuck up if I do?"

"Yeah. Whatever."

"Tell her I got . . . a '72 Challenger . . . with a hemi . . . Ask her if she . . . wants that."

"Does it run?"

"Does it run."

"Well, does it?"

"You never seen . . . anything like it . . . The Roadrunner, either . . . Got some rust . . . in the doors . . . and the trunk . . . a little around the . . . windshield . . . Interior's fucked up . . . It's a monster though . . . But I'm sick of . . . fuckin' with it . . . Give it to her."

"Hey, Mazzie? Yeah. He wants to let you have this totally monster muscle car . . . He says he's got a lot in the motor, but it needs a little body work . . . Well, if you need one, take it . . . Yeah, you can drive it away . . . Tonight . . . I know . . . Look, this is an emergency . . . I know . . . Yeah . . . Totally . . . I totally understand. You're a professional . . . Why don't you just come take a look? . . . You will? . . . Thank you so much. You are so cool . . . Okay . . . Okay, we're out on Airline at . . . Oh, yeah, I forgot you knew him . . . Okay. You know where to find us . . . When you comin'? All right . . . All right, bye."

"I can't believe . . . that slut . . . is coming out . . . to exorcise my . . . demons."

"Dude! Do *not* talk like that about Mazzie. It's really dangerous. She's got power."

"Whatever," said Snake.

"Dude, your attitude is really fucked up. Don't you have any spirituality at all?" asked Tania.

Before dawn, Mazzie showed up in a '74 Econoline van. Munchy just about knocked the trailer door down as he raised the alarm, waking Snake and Tania. They barely heard the knocking on the door over the basso barking. Tania commanded Munchy to hush, and the dog sulked over to the couch, where he lay back down. Tania opened the door. Mazzie stood outside the door, a fat woman of about thirty-five with fine, pale skin and thick-lensed, black-framed glasses, their clumsy frames held together on the left side with masking tape. She wore a vaguely medieval-looking gray tunic over a long black skirt, and her smell was like that of old marijuana in shag carpet mixed with the scent of plug-in air fresheners. Mazzie squinted, trying to focus on Tania. The effort made her show her top teeth and double the amount of gums.

"Hi, Mazzie."

"Damn," she said with a Mississippi accent, "there's a war going on in here."

"Really?"

"I don't fool around, babe. How's the eyebrow?" Tania raised her hand to her eyebrow ring, which Mazzie had installed the year before with a large sterilized lance and a cork.

"It was infected for a couple months, but it's just great now. No problems."

"I told you you'd have to keep it clean. You didn't keep up with the Phisohex, did you?" said Mazzie as she labored to enter the trailer.

"I guess I didn't really take care of it like I should have. I didn't have my shit together back then."

"It takes a long time. Hey, Snake."

"Fuck," he replied.

"Okay, let's see what we got here." She looked around the place, sniffed, held her arms out with her palms vertical, and did a 360. "The first thing you gotta do is git every one of these posters down what got any Satanic shit on 'em and pile 'em outside. Then you go through all his magazines and books— look under his bed, too—and pile any Satanic shit or porno out in the same pile."

Tania pulled down a Megadeth poster first, and then ripped a Sepulcher poster off the wall. Marilyn Manson came next, and just to be safe she also removed the Nine Inch Nails poster. Snake didn't have much in the way of books, but, just like Mazzie had suggested, a pile of porno mags sat under the bed. She checked a few of them out, though, because she hadn't ever really seen any hard-core porno before, and got interested in trying to find the story line in *Cum Sluts #6* because the guy had a big dragon tattoo. As she started leafing through *Oral Angels,* she gave a negative grunt and threw the whole pile out with the rest. Tania worked while Mazzie sat on the couch and gave herself a man's manicure. The ceramic bong with the demon and the pentagram definitely had to go. Mazzie waved her index finger at it saying, "Over here, honey." After all the offending materials had been removed, Mazzie lifted herself up from the couch, lit four white candles on the coffee table, and turned out the light.

"Forces of darkness, git thee away from this mobile home," she began. "Honey, go git me them branches out the back o' the van, and don't wake Buster." Tania went out to get the branches. Over her shoulder she heard Mazzie saying, "Forces of darkness, the game is over. Go ask your fellow demons about me. They'll tell you 'bout Mazzie Wilson. You're wastin' your time tryin' to stick around 'cause I ain't leavin till you release your hold on all the energy and stuff in this trailer. Especially get your hooks outa that man, Snake, over there. I know you thought he was easy, but he just got help." She pulled out a purple Crown Royal bag. Out of the bag, she pulled a plastic bag sealed with a twist tie. She opened it and grabbed a palm full of white powder, which she began to toss around, creating a chalky haze. Then she began to light incense sticks and place them around the room. Within a minute or two, the atmosphere had become unbreathable. Snake began to cough. "I told you, get thee away," hollered Mazzie. Tania returned with the branches.

"Is he all right?" asked Tania, who had heard Snake coughing.

"That's the demons comin' out of him. He's in the purifyin' process."

"Open a window," begged Snake.

"You'll get an open window soon enough," said Mazzie taking the branches from Tania and beating Snake with them mercilessly. "Out! Out!" she screamed.

"Cut it out. You get . . . the fuck out," said Snake. "I just want to die . . . in peace." Tania looked on from a corner, having second thoughts about Mazzie, who was flailing away at the fetal ball under the unzipped sleeping-bag that Snake used for a blanket. The whole scene seemed like a nightmare to Tania, with Mazzie's jiggling bulk waving branches around in the candle-lit haze of the trailer.

"Okay! Tania!" barked Mazzie like a drill sergeant. "Go get the gas can from the van and set that shit on fire! Hurry!" Tania hurried out of the trailer. As she stepped out into the night, she heard Mazzie bellow, "And don't wake Buster!" Tania rushed to the back of the van and quietly opened the rear door. The plastic gasoline container sat just inside the door, and Tania grabbed it, afraid of the loud snoring emanating from the blackness of the van's interior. "This is bullshit," she muttered. She had gotten frustrated and angry at Mazzie for barking at her and whipping Snake. *I'll just get this over with. I'm never calling that bitch again. She can't even pierce an eyebrow right.*

She rushed over and poured the gas onto the pile of crumpled posters, magazines, records, and small objects obscured in the darkness. With her disposable lighter, she lit a small piece of paper and dropped it onto the pile. The pile ignited with a lot more heat and violence than she had expected, singing the hair on her arms and her eyebrows. She screamed not because of the explosion, but because of the demonic forms she saw reaching toward her out of the flames. She backed up quickly, heart pounding, legs turning to rubber. Then the fire began to look like any other fire, and she tried to catch her breath.

"Fuck! I gotta get some sleep," said Tania to herself. She backed up toward the trailer, then went inside. Mazzie lay exhausted and breathing heavily on the sofa, and Snake lay curled up in a ball under the sleeping bag. "Are you done?" asked Tania.

Mazzie looked over in Tania's direction, her eyes not good enough to actually make her out in the darkness.

"No. Just gimme a second, okay?"

"Okay."

Then, with great labor, Mazzie got up out of the sofa and walked over to Snake.

"Snake! Wake up! I gotta finish this, but this part ain't gonna be so bad. I promise." Mazzie pulled on the sleeping bag, but he clutched it tightly over his head, so she had to yank.

"Get off me. God damn you, Mazzie."

"We gotta get him up and put him in the shower. Now don't try to fight me, Snake. You know you're gonna lose. You know that, right, honey?"

"Mazzie, really . . . I can't stand up . . . You gotta leave me . . . alone."

"Tania, go get that bag of oranges out one of them grocery bags in the van and squeeze him a glass of juice. We gotta get his sugar up."

"That'll go right through him."

"I bet he'll hold it now. Git it. An' don't wake Buster."

☉☉☉

Snake finished the juice. "How's that, boy?" asked Tania.

"That's really good. I feel a . . . little better."

"You gotta walk, now." Mazzie managed to get him stripped and to his feet. Tania stared, shocked at Snake's appearance. He looked like a concentration camp prisoner—not much more than a skeleton, especially with the lights now on and with him standing supported by Mazzie's bulk. "Get that shower runnin' hot, Tania. He's got to get in water before this is over."

They stood him up in the shower and washed his whole body as Mazzie intoned prayers. Strange spasms began to wrack Snake's body, and he began to belch and cough up stuff. Mazzie said it was more spirits coming out. They dried him and put him in bed again, and Tania listened to his breathing for a minute or two. It seemed less strained and shallow. She turned toward Mazzie, who stood by the door.

"You really did something to him."

"Wasn't me, baby," said Mazzie with a husky laugh, "but I could still use the car."

"Sure. I got the keys here. Here you go."

"Let's go out and check it out."

Munchy, who had finally come out from behind the couch, followed them out as they walked outside past the smoldering, molten, black spot where the fire had been. Mazzie pounded on the side of the van. "Buster! Wake up, Buster!" They heard the back doors open up, and Buster came around. He had a rough face, long stringy hair, and cheap tattoos visible all up his arms in the light of the pre-dawn sky. "This is Tania. She's one of mine." Anyone Mazzie ever pierced was one of "hers."

"Hey, Mama," said Buster nodding to the rhythm of whatever was playing inside his head. His smile revealed a large space where his two front teeth had once been.

"Hey," said Tania.

"Go start that car up," said Mazzie, and handed Buster the keys. Buster smelled like pot as he walked toward the Challenger.

"Mazzie, like, you were great," said Tania. "I don't know what to say. It was really intense. I mean, I can feel he's getting a lot better."

"Just don't let him fuck around. As soon as he can, you get him started on that tattoo 'cause he's liable to croak on you." Buster tried the starter, but the Challenger wouldn't fire up. He had to pop the hood and use a splash of gasoline from what remained in the bottom of the gas can to prime the carburetor.

"Hell, baby! This a parful motah! You betta let me drav it!"

"That's *my* car, Buster! You just start it!" He tried the ignition with the primed carb, and it started with a startling racket.

"Ha! It works," hollered Mazzie over the thunder of the Challenger. "Okay, Tania, I got to go get me some sleep."

"I just don't know how to thank you," yelled Tania and gave Mazzie a hug.

"Okay, we're gone, sweety." With that, Mazzie and Buster drove off with the van and the Challenger. Soon the quiet restored itself.

Tania went back inside the trailer.

"Snake. You awake?"

"Yeah. I feel like I . . . might be getting over the hump here."

"I told you she had power. I saw demons coming out of your shit when it burned up."

"Whatever. Now I'm just gonna have to . . . go through all that again. Maybe you should just let me die."

"No. I'm not gonna let you," said Tania. "You've got something to live for."

"What? I don't have shit."

Tania got up from the little couch, stood by the bed, and held her arms out, exposing the anaconda.

"Show me the whole thing." Tania, with an air of significance, took her T-shirt off and turned around so he could see the way the snake slithered over her shoulders. She held her arms out, palms toward Snake, and began to make undulating, snake-like motions with her arms.

"Turn around." She turned. Her breasts stood there like open pearly gates—sublime, full, radiating life, it seemed to Snake. "God, Tania . . . I never thought . . . I'd see anything . . . that fine again." She danced gracefully, as if made of feathers or eels. Then she took off the rest of her clothes and continued to dance as Snake watched, transfixed. He wanted nothing but to get up out of the bed and go to her, but all he could do was lie there. A tent started to rise in the sheets. Tania got a rubber out of her purse, then returned, and put it on Snake. She got in bed, guided a breast to his mouth, and started to jerk him off. When he came, she felt tears between her breasts.

"There you go, baby. Mama's here."

❍❍❍

Snake, the stick figure, started work on the tattoo the next day. He got out of bed at around three in the afternoon and dug his equipment out of a plastic tackle box, putting it on the little coffee table in front of the couch. Munchy stared at him from the foot of the bed, looking guilty for having slept inside. Snake looked back at him, genuinely glad to see him—genuinely glad to see anything. He held his tattoo gun up and said, "Yeah." Tania rustled around under the covers on the bed.

"Wake up! You're mine!" he said.

"What? What time is it?"

"It's time for you to get your snake, my pretty piece of flesh."

"Don't call me that."

"Get up, girl." Tania didn't move. Snake decided to try a different tack. "I think I feel a little dizzy," he said. Tania got up to make him some orange juice and cut up some bananas.

After Snake ate breakfast, he went to work on her, explaining that he had to have her topless as he worked in order to "get the slither of the snake harmonized with the stymmetry of your morphology," and the needle buzzed all afternoon across Tania's shoulder. He didn't spend much time looking at her breasts, but he liked the idea that they were there for emergencies. His closeness to death seemed to somehow fixate his psyche on them, but he concentrated hard upon his work, eyes ready to pop out from the strain of concentration as he worked on each scale of the tattoo. His face got red and a little sweaty as he worked.

Snake was one of the new school of tattooists. Instead of putting the ink in deep, where the years would blur it more, he used a fine needle, and only placed the ink shallowly under her skin so the tattoo would remain sharply detailed into Tania's old age, though he couldn't imagine her seeing her thirtieth birthday.

After the first session, Snake looked enervated, and Tania went to work at the Goddess. Snake had thought about writing a will for a long time, and finally sat down to write it on a piece of blue lined paper. When Tania got home again at three in the morning, Snake told her to take off her shirt so he could start again.

"I just got home from work, dude. Gimme a break," she said.

"Girl, I gotta get my needle in you again. Don't ask any questions. I don't have forever like you do, remember?" He lifted her shirt over her breasts and moved the palms of his hands in a circular motion over her subtly-defined nipples.

"Dude," she said, frustrated.

"I don't even know what I want. Look, just put your ass down on that couch and let me get to work on the fucking tat, or I'm gonna get horny or freak out or something."

"I don't have to do anything, dude. You're working for me, remember?"

"Yeah, I know. Just don't start thinking it's only worth twelve hundred bucks. This is the most intense detail I've ever seen—on any tattoo ever."

"I know, dude, why'd you fucking have to make it like that? I mean, it's really fine, but I never expected *anything* like this. It's like way over the top."

"I needed something that would take a while and keep you coming around."

"Huh!" she said, shaking her head. "I can't believe you've been using me like that, bastard. I thought this was about art."

"Well, what the fuck is art about?"

"I was right. You're really not spiritual at all, dude."

"Look," said Snake, his face reddening, "you're the one that came to me for your fucking tattoo. Why? 'Cause I was good, that's why. You needed something *from* me. So why are you cutting me because I want something from you? Huh? You just think everyone should just work for you for free cause you think you're spiritual or some shit?"

"No, dude! But I'm doing shit for you that's worth way more than twelve hundred dollars, too. I'm taking care of you, and cleaning up after you when you're sick. You'd be dead now if it wasn't for me!"

Snake left a long silence, and his response came quietly.

"I know that, girl. So why are you cutting me 'cause I want to keep you around? You're keeping me alive, and you inspire me, you know? So why am I such a dog 'cause I want you?" Tania's expression softened. She hugged him.

"Oh, you can be so sweet sometimes, dude. Okay," she said, and removed her shirt. She took his hands and backed up to the couch.

"Can you, like, get your pants off, too. I'm getting to the point that I really need to check out how the tattoo looks with the rest of your body."

"You're getting to the point where you want to see me naked, dude. That's what it is," she said stripping off her leather pants and exposing white cotton panties with pink hearts. Snake got hard.

"Girl, you are so fine." Tania tried not to smile, failed, and shook her head again. She felt almost maternal about Snake, as if he were a perpetually innocent toddler running around with a hard-on. She sat down on the couch and started to stroke him through his loose jeans as he stood in front of her. She rummaged in her purse, pulled out a grape-flavored condom, unzipped him, and put it on him. "I'm tired, so make it quick," she said, and gave him a blow job. They then went to bed, and he again fell asleep between her breasts.

AUTHOR: Weren't you afraid he'd give you AIDS?

Prytania Relf: I made sure he always had a rubber on.

A: Yeah, but still . . .

PR: But what? Like I'm gonna deny a dying artist his last wishes? I don't think so.

A: Tania, he fucking had AIDS. And not only were you doing him, you let him stick a needle under your skin.

PR: Dude, what is your fucking problem? Look, the needle was sterilized. How the fuck am I supposed to get AIDS from a sterilized needle? You know what you are, dude? You're one of those motherfuckers that pretends to be cool, but you aren't. You prob'ly make fun of dumbasses that think you can get it from like touching, but you're just like 'em. Well, I'm not. The doctors say you can't get it from touching or sterile needles, and that's good enough. I am not going to avoid people with it like it's a plague or some shit like that. That is the most ignorant and cruel fucked-up shit, dude. It's is none of your fucking business what I do, anyhow. You just don't understand. I thought you did, but you don't.

A: I just think it's a little out of the ordinary that you'd have sex with a guy with AIDS. Why're you getting so pissed?

PR: You're judging me. You are just so fucking small, dude. You think I'm just like some crazy bitch, but if you could see through my eyes, you'd get to see somethin' beautiful that you're never gonna get to see in your whole life.

A: Like what?

PR: Like, even if I was a roach, and I could see somethin' beautiful, I'd still be better off than you are, dude, 'cause you don't know somethin' beautiful when you see it. You're just a closed-up jerk. [Laugh] You made it sound like you were all sensitive n' shit when you were tryin' to get me to tell the story, and now you're just turning into some like football player, or somethin'. You're not a writer. No wonder you can't get any work. Fuck you bye. [Tania gets up and heads for the door.]

A: Well, where is the beautiful fucking story here, then, huh? All I'm getting is some dreadlock-slut sucking off some AIDS-infected tattoo artist in a trailer park. [At this point, Tania rushes back, gives me the flat of her hand across the side of my head, and knocks me off my mattress.] Bitch! [Tania continues to come at me—swinging, and landing blows. I throw her down on my mattress, sit on her butt, and pin her, facedown, hands behind her back. In this position, I continue the interview.] Just chill out, Tania. Jesus!

PR: Get off, you asshole!

A: Quit screaming, goddamn it! You're gonna get the cops up here! [She quiets down quickly. At this point I notice that her hips are slightly and rhythmically thrusting into the mattress.] Okay, I'm gonna let you go now. I'm sorry, okay? I didn't mean all that shit. I'm just still on edge, you know. You gonna hit me if I let you go?[Twenty-two seconds of silence]

PR: Please . . .

A: Please what? [Fifteen seconds of silence]

PR: Just hold me like this for a while, okay? [This line is whispered, so it's illegible on the tape. I am, however, pretty sure those were her exact words.]

A: Okay. [She continues her subtle thrusting, her cheeks turn the most delicate shade of pink, and she begins to breathe heavily. Eventually the movement ceases.]

PR: Let me go, dude.

A: Yeah. Okay. [I let her go, she rolls over on her back,

and I get a drink of spring water out of the refrigerator. This takes place during a minute and thirty-eight seconds of silence on tape.]

PR: When he was working on my arm, I used to look at him staring at me—concentrating really hard. Even when he was getting really sick again, and he had like a 105-degree fever, he'd still stare so hard and concentrate so hard—even when you could tell the life was like burning out of him. I swear the tat even got better, the closer he got to dying. [Holds up her arm showing the tattoo from the back of her left hand to her elbow.] This is where he started to get sick again. [Points at a spot three inches below her elbow] And this is where he finished it. [Points at the tip of the tail on her middle knuckle. There does seem to be more intense definition of detail, the closer it gets to the tip of the tail.] See, you don't understand. Like when you get a real artist workin' on you, it's intense. It's just you, and him, and the needle, and forever, and like the needle is connected right to the art and my skin and to him and to me—burning into me like it feels like his eyes are burning into me and this beautiful snake is just slithering out of mid-air—you know what I mean?—out of the space between us, but it connects us, too. It's like havin' a mind-child. It's much more intense than fucking. Like, all the walls are gone—he's piercing my skin and it fucking hurts. It really hurts. He's in me, escaping into me, and the art is in me, and I'm protecting them both. When somethin' like that happens, you just feel like making the other person happy, you know? You have to grab onto that moment, 'cause you don't get many of those times in life. Most people prob'ly never get one moment like that. I'm not gonna be Miss Priss and not let Snake be happy because I might *might* get sick. You gotta take chances, or you're nothing. You wouldn't expect a nurse to do that, would you—just refuse to touch a dying guy? No, dude. They put on their rubber gloves and help him, but you know what? They'd do it if they didn't have gloves, too. You think Mother Theresa wouldn't touch a leper 'cause he was sick? He's a human being, with feelings, and love. I know it sounds funny that Snake had love in him, but he really really did. Like, he was willing to put his entire self into it—into me, you know, and he had the balls to do it without asking for anything or promising anything—you know—like a buggy horse with blinds on. He wouldn't look at the future, or the past—he just wanted . . . me. Right in the moment. Not some dream, or some like act. Me. Now. He was so beautiful.

A: You must have been upset when he died.

PR: I guess so.

A: How did he go?

PR: Well, he couldn't really move much, toward the end, and I had to take care of him like all the time. He didn't really sleep or wake up after while. And I had to keep changin' him. The smell was really bad. Then he started getting really de-hydrated, and he stopped messing himself. I had to lie on the bed, while he was lying on his side next to me working on me. He was really really hot. I was working on so little sleep that I actually went to sleep while he was workin' on me. I dreamed about a snake with wings, I shit you not, and when I woke up, I looked down at my arm and it was finished! I was like "Dude! Dude! You finished it!" but he wasn't hot anymore.

(Taped conversation: 1996)

chapter 11.
WILL

I SNAKE BEING OF SOUND MIND AND BODY BECUETH MY DOG
*Munchy to Tania. The rest of the mony she ows me and everything
elce like the car and the trailer has to be used to get me creamated
and for this party I want her to throw for me and my freinds. It has
got to be held some place big with an out side part, and it has to be
advertized. There has to be go go girls in cages waring Cathlic school
girl outfits with short skirts so everybody can see there under ware
and loud music that people can dance to. Personaly I like rock and
roll but you cant dance to it so just play something funky. I want
Tomasso to DJ even though he is a mother fucker, Tomasso, and he
ows me $900 anyway, remember Tomasso? You beter D J for free ass
hole. The tattoo I put on Tania is the most fucking awesome tattoo I
ever did. There has to be an announcemint that my masterpeice is
going to be unvaled, and then Tania has to show it to every body.
Any body that lets my sister bury me in Ohio is going to get their ass
kicked, caus I will make a special trip back to fuck them up. Im not
kiding. She cant have my ashes, either. You hear that Lizzy? And I
don't want you at my party sober either. If you come to my party,
you better not be acting like your all holyer then thow. Tania will be
in charge of making shure she gets loded. Marcus can come, but hes
got to keep his urotrash hands off Tania. If he starts hitting on her
hes out. Any questions about that Marcus? Have I ben clear enuf?
Tania is in charge of the party, and if she can get all this shit done,
she can keep half of what's left over. My sister gets the other half of
whatever is left over. You can suprise me about what you do with my
ashes, but try to make it creativ, Tania. Snake.*

chapter 12.
AT THE COFFEEHOUSE

BIG MARCUS AND TOMASSO WERE AT THE CAFÉ. HUSHED SAMBA reverberated between the stone-tiled floor and the high, molded-tin ceiling until the music became almost unidentifiable. The scarce light in the space came from abstract neon art installations on the walls or in the plate glass windows, and the dimness of the café seemed to amplify the swimmy acoustic ambience. Art hung on all of the walls and stood in corners. On slow weeknights like this one, when, regardless of the heat, more coffee passed over the bar than alcohol, only the hiss of the espresso machine's milk steamer broke the relative quiet.

Tomasso placed a demitasse on the table. The tiny cup was half full of the blackest Bustello available in town, just below a thin layer of orange-brown crema. He picked up the sugar container and poured until the coffee came up to the rim. Then he stirred the stuff until the sugar dissolved. One sip took care of half of it. Another took care of the rest.

"She's hardly spoken to me in weeks," complained Marcus. "She's been holed up with Snake the whole time, and now that he's dead, she still hasn't come to see me. I go to see her at the Goddess, and she just says a quick hello or waves. I ask her if I can visit her, and she makes excuses. And I haven't even seen the bloody tattoo now that it's finished." Marcus gulped some of his black, unsweetened café Americano, which had gone lukewarm.

"You'll get to see the tattoo at the party like everybody

else. She's been non-stop for weeks. Maybe she just hasn't had time to deal with you. Do you know how taxing it is to organize a party like this?"

"Oh yes. Snake's still a pain in the arse in death, but, look—I'm the one who has to make the flyers for the party, and I don't even get kissed."

"You're acting like a schoolgirl," snapped Tomasso. "Everyone is doing something. Herman's welding go-go-girl cages out of scrap metal, so don't complain about making flyers."

"But Herman loves this sort of thing."

"*You* love this kind of thing," Tomasso said, raising his voice. "This kind of thing is the only reason you stay around here. You're just bitching about your unfair mistress. If you don't want anything to do with it, then don't come. Otherwise, just shut up, and pitch in like everyone else."

"There would be no bloody party if I hadn't pinched that money from Gator and broke Snake out of Charity," Marcus mumbled.

"Listen. Just drop it. Why are you always obsessing over her?"

"They used to have a thing called love, Tomasso. It's similar to a substance abuse problem, so you should be able to grasp the concept. You see someone, and you want her. You can't stop thinking of her, and you consider desperate things like monogamy, homeownership, children, and the thought of these measures failing seems like a cosmic tragedy. No matter what you . . ."

"You just keep talking. It's amazing. You're like an old lady going on about her cat. Nobody could possibly be interested."

"I'm sorry. I'm just trying to understand how overwhelmed I feel with beauty—why I can't seem to deal with it."

"The reason you can't handle beauty is that you think too much about it. That's all it is. Some dreadlocked bim shows up—with, granted, a very nice pair—and your head gets all wound up. You're just in love with your own mind."

"No. I am in love with her. Once, when I was a child, I saw a Vermeer in the Louvre of a woman in a window, and I just stood there staring at it for the longest time. It felt like the light flooding into the room in the painting and the woman in the window were more real than me, and when I came back to myself, I felt intense grief. I wanted to stay in the painting with her forever. Now Tania's the Vermeer to me. She's become the canvas for her own visions. How could I not love her more than any painting, when all the great works of art are just attempts at conveying the feeling I get when I'm with her? She's what I've been trying to get back to ever since that day I had to walk away from the painting."

"Oh, I hear accordion music!" said Tomasso, cupping his hand to his ear. His voice sounded breathless. "Are those dancing midgets?" he asked and whipped his hand up as if to shade his eyes. "Wait. I think I've seen this one before. Ingmar Birdbrain. The Unbearable Lightness of Betty. Skinny Betty. Betty the lezzie!" said Tomasso. "Where is Betty when you need her, anyway? "

"You are not overly affected by beauty and love, are you, Tomasso?"

"I invented Betty, didn't I? Look, Marcus. I see a beautiful painting, and I want to hang it on my wall and snort crystal with my back to it. I see a beautiful dame, and I want to bounce her on my knee and tell dirty jokes in Japanese."

"Very romantic."

"Romance: an exercise whereby one surrenders his judgement to a less-trustworthy party. Sound familiar?"

Marcus remained quiet then, but he knew that when or if he grew old and thought back on his years in New Orleans, Tania would encapsulate the whole thing—her animated, dreadlock-framed smile, her stainless steel studs and rings in the glistening numb darkness of a crowded lounge, the cigarette-scented flowers of corruption, the perfection of the exact wrong thing. It all reeked of beauty, ached with awareness, died as you kissed it, a crumbling goddess.

He knew he wanted a love from her she couldn't give, even if she were to spread her legs for him. She was simply not capable of it, he thought. He certainly could not give her what she needed from a man, which was thoughtless action, a washboard stomach, and a cock like a loaf of French bread. Yet between them seemed to form a strange union of opposites in Marcus's mind. *My God, if I didn't love her so much, she might be what Tomasso and everyone else seems to think she is.* He found the thought almost unfathomable.

Marcus sat silent until a pair of arms wrapped around him from behind. He looked down and saw a completed snake tattoo sticking its head and tail out past the cuffs of a long-sleeved undershirt.

"I've been looking all over for you, dude," said Tania. He turned his head sideways, and found himself lost in dreadlocks for a moment as Tania kissed his mouth. The universe became hollow, light, filled with xenon gas. Then she went over to Tomasso, and kissed him on the lips, too. The xenon gas dissipated. She sat down at the table with them.

"I'm so glad to see you guys. Listen. Snake's bitch, church-lady sister showed up at the trailer this morning and went postal when she saw me in there. Started fucking screaming at me to get out—after all I did for him. Anyway, she wants to take Snake back to Wisconsin or Iowa or wherever the bumfuck she's from to bury him, and you read the will, dude. I can't let her do it, or fucked up shit's gonna happen." Marcus took a sip of his coffee, not wanting to hear any of what she had to say.

"That's just their custom on the great plains—part of their religion," said Tomasso. "Just let it go. You're not going to change her mind."

"I basically don't give a fuck about her mind, dude. It's her brother's body I'm worried about. Here's my plan—"

"No, no, no," said Marcus quickly. "No plans."

"Come on, dude! I need help. I've got this, like, plan. OK? Tonight we go get his body out of the coroner's." She stopped speaking.

Marcus looked at her and said "That is not a plan! Plans have details, Tania. They show forethought and consideration of contingencies. That is a disaster, not a plan. I'll bet you don't even know where the morgue is, do you?"

"Good thing I didn't listen to you about getting Snake out of the hospital, dude. I'd have never got my tat finished. You are so fucking negative. I'm gonna do it whether you fucking help or not. Tomasso'll help me out. Won't you?"

"Well, that seems a little bit crazy when you consider the risks. For instance, legal fees, prison, getting my skinny white ass auctioned off for packs of cigarettes."

"That's not gonna happen, dude, but I understand. I know you're not in this. I just thought Marcus cared."

"And what are you going to do about the body when you get it?" asked Marcus. "You can't just walk into a funeral parlor with a body and say 'Cremate this.' I do care, Tania, but not to the point of abject stupidity."

"So I'm a stupid object?"

"Excuse me, lovebirds," said Tomasso. He had spotted Marilyn and Little Marcus through the window as they passed by. "I need to go talk to some friends."

"Okay, dude," said Tania to Tomasso, who had already gotten up. When Tomasso made it out to the sidewalk, he noticed that Little Marcus and Marilyn, who had just passed, seemed enmeshed in a serious conversation. Marilyn's raised chin, and Little Marcus's low, deliberate voice and hand gestures—palms up, hands slowly rising and falling—told Tomasso he should not butt in. He sat down at one of the tables outside. Marilyn always brightened up his outlook with her starlet inflections and girlish wit. He decided he would go home shortly, as he had grown bored with everyone in the coffee house—on the entire street, in fact—maybe the world. At home he would play with his synthesizer, and try to use his electric toothbrush as a musical instrument in some way, possibly by turning it on and raking it across the strings of his electric guitar. All hope of good conversation faded as Marilyn and Little Marcus drew further away.

"Our relationship is stagnating, Marcus," said Marilyn. "It was just so beautiful at the beginning, and I'll always cherish that, but you have to realize that my feelings are no reflection on you as a person. Don't you realize, dear, how huge a burden it is to be the sole vindication of another person's life? There are lots of beautiful things in life, and lots of people to love. You act like I am the only light on a darkened soundstage, and—"

"Marilyn, listen. You really don't know about what the f . . . what my life is like, and I know you are very delicate, but let me tell you I'm a twisted little 34-year-old dwarf, inside and out. A dwarf, a dwarf, a dwarf. Do you understand what the f . . . what that means? Brats point at me every time I go out in the daylight, guys stare at me when I'm not looking at them, and look away when I look back. I walk around dreaming of torturing those perfect bastards. But I don't have the guts, so I have to settle for those little faggots in the bathtub at Hurley's who figure the most nastiest thing in the world is to get pissed on by Little Marcus—me. They brag about getting pissed on by Little Marcus. So I piss on 'em, and make 'em lick my boots, and my—"

"Marcus. Stop it. Please, stop it!"

"I'm sorry, Marilyn. I don't mean to use that language in front of you."

"Please, don't go on anymore. This is just the kind of thing that scares me about you."

"I know, Marilyn, but this is me without you. I don't want to go back to that. I thought you were the one person who would understand me. Now you want to leave, and just so you can see other guys who could never feel the way I do about you."

"That is not why! That is not why, Marcus."

"I thought you'd stay with me like in all those movies. You wouldn't even have to stay with me long, 'cause people like me don't live too long anyway. If I live ten years, it'll be a miracle. Before you, I always thought I'd die alone with nobody at the funeral. And that's a dream, too, Marilyn, because there ain't even gonna be no funeral anyway, and I ain't gonna have you with me when I die. But, for something like a year now, I've been seeing you announce the shows, and when I see you in the spot, you're so alive. It's not just your dresses; you sparkle inside, too. You glitter more inside than your sequins do in a spotlight. I made a total idiot of myself when I went to you, just because you were the greatest thing in my life, and I told you because I hoped . . . I don't know what, and then it was like a miracle when you felt something for me, and all these emotions started coming out of me—out of me! Regular feelings! Normal feelings! For the first time in my life I felt like a human being, not a freak faggot, so don't tell me about all these wonderful things that are going to happen to me in the future, and all the other chances I'm going to get for being happy. Don't lie to me or yourself. If you leave me, I'm fucked forever. Nobody'll ever lo . . . love you like me. I want to marry you—get a domestic partnership, everything."

"Marcus, I can't—no. I have to be alone now. I'm going home the rest of the way alone. Don't follow me. I have to go now."

"Marilyn! Marilyn!" croaked Marcus.

"Stop it!" cried six feet two inches, and two hundred and seventy pounds of Marilyn as she trotted off, her strides abbreviated by her tight, sequined dress.

Little Marcus directed his tortured wobble-walk toward Hurley's.

◎◎◎

"Abject, not object," said Big Marcus.

"Hey, I went to New Orleans public school, not your stuck-up British schools, but I know what stupid means. What is with you, dude? You're on the rag every time I talk to you," said Tania.

Marcus took another sip of coffee.

"Dude, is this the silent treatment? It better not be the silent treatment. I can play that."

"If I say anything, I'll just make a damned fool of myself, so I think I'll just not talk," said Marcus.

"Dude, it can't be too hard to get a body out of the morgue."

"The difficulty hardly strikes me as the principal issue. The sanity of the thing seems to be the question. Shall we get Sarge to come along as well, darling?"

"Just fuck you." Tania stood up quickly and walked out the door. With a supreme effort to salvage his self-respect, Marcus let her walk out without any protest or apology. As Tania charged into the night air, she saw Tomasso sitting at a table.

"He is really pissing me off, dude. I don't need his shit anymore."

"Yeah. It's cool. I think your relationship has outlasted its usefulness, anyway. He's been saying how sick he is of your complications, too."

"What did he say? I can't believe he's been talking about me behind my back. What did he say?"

"Be cool. It was nothing, really. He hasn't really been talking about you much anymore, at all. He was just saying how he was getting over that stupid crush that's been annoying you so much, and he's feeling better now that he doesn't feel so involved in your tattoo project anymore. Just leave him alone for a week or two, and I think he'll stop bothering you. As his friend, I feel I really should apologize for his making such an ass of himself. He just gets obsessed every now and then. I just want you to know he can really be Joe Coolbreeze. He's starting to get obsessed with Betty, now, anyway. So you won't have to bother with him anymore."

"What a relief," said Tania, surprised, "I've been trying to explain that I just don't get that feeling from him, you know. I tried to let him down easy."

"Yeah. I know. You've been really cool, and it's paying off. I mean, he's got to figure it out when you're paying more attention to a dead guy!" Tomasso laughed. Tania laughed a little halfheartedly along with him.

"God. That's such a load off my mind, dude. So, uh—who's this Betty?" said Tania, her left eye twitching ever so minutely.

"She's quite a beautiful and talented thespian—completely out of his league, but she doesn't know it."

"I feel so much better, dude. I guess I'll hang out for a while. I could use some coffee."

"I'm going home. Marilyn and Little Marcus just left, and

I'm a little depressed about it. I thought I was going to get some of her effervescent conversation. By the way . . . about tomorrow . . . when she emcees the party, you really need to flatter her, and don't be conservative about it. You can lay it on as thick as you want, and she'll never guess you're buttering her buns. You could have problems with her if you don't make her feel pretty and appreciated."

"Okay, dude. Thanks."

"I'm off to the bat cave. Hold all my calls." Tomasso kissed Tania on the lips and walked off toward his apartment.

"Later, Tomasso," said Tania standing there alone on the sidewalk. She walked back in toward the counter, taking care not to look in Marcus's direction, and ordered an iced cappuccino. Skinny, 18-year-old Tessa, with her long, brown hair and long, hippie skirt struggled at depressing the piston handle of the old brass Italian-made espresso machine until it yielded enough espresso to make an iced cap. As Tessa began to froth the milk, Tania stole a few looks over in Marcus's direction in the mirror behind the bar. He simply sat there with his forehead in his hand appearing to survey the club listings in a magazine.

In actuality, he struggled against the urge to go over and talk to Tania, and he had no real awareness of what magazine he appeared to be reading. He simply knew it was a magazine, and that he looked as if he were reading it. The tension built up inside him to do something, though he wanted to just sit there and ignore her. He had to do something. All he knew was he would try his best to salvage some dignity by not going over to talk to her. He opted to leave saying to himself simply, *Fuck it. This is ridiculous. Tania is, from now on, a lost love.* He got up and walked out the door.

Tessa served Tania her iced cap just as Tania spied Marcus leaving. Tania felt a little queasy in her lower abdomen as she stared at her cappuccino. The darkness of the espresso at the top slowly descended and writhed, ruining the perfect, cold white of the ice and milk. She couldn't identify the feeling in her gut. It seemed to have elements of resentment, sexual longing, anger, helplessness, despair, hatred, and hope. She saw images of her father rejecting her, and images of her mother walking away toward the car. Tania all of a sudden imagined what Betty might look like, and imagined Marcus on his way to her. She charged out of the door after Marcus as the cappuccino stood there untouched.

"Marcus! Wait up!" she yelled when she got within earshot of him as he walked up Decatur Street. Marcus turned. When he saw it was her, he kept walking. She began to run, catching up with him just before he made it to his apartment house door.

"Marcus, what is your *fuck*ing problem?"

Marcus continued to walk toward his door, as Tania dogged him.

"What did I do? I thought we were friends, dude. I'm sorry."

He put the key in the iron barred door to the courtyard of his building, turned the lock, and opened the door.

"Tania, I know I don't know what to say, and I don't want to talk, at any rate. I'm sure we'll see each other after we've cooled for a while. Let's keep this simple." He entered the gate.

"You weren't ever my friend, anyway," said Tania. "You just wanted a piece of me."

Marcus prepared to say something, but simply closed the gate and walked down the long brick hall toward the courtyard. Tania experienced a flood of emotions and images, and felt a renewed and more profound void in her belly. She saw her father closing the door on her, many different times, and her mother at various stages of her last walk to the car.

Images of the inside of Marcus's apartment came to her

with a sugary glow of nostalgia. She remembered it now as a holy sanctuary. Marcus then seemed like a patient and benevolent presence that had extended an unnoticed and impenetrable protection around her, and now he was walking away from her. Some tiny part of her consciousness that did not find itself in utter turmoil realized that she was hitting herself in the head over and over again.

"No!" she shrieked, throwing herself against the metal bars. The sound resonated against the brick like the scream of a falcon. "Please! Don't go!" Marcus had never even heard anything like it even in the slasher movies he had studied in the film course "Transgression and Perversity in the Body Metaphor." But this cry shocked the ear more than a slasher queen. The timbre of it shot through the consciousness like a bullet through a picture tube. He spun around. "Marcus!" she cried plaintively and softly this time. Marcus had never heard his name said like that—ever. It was repulsively syrupy yet extremely erotic in its devotion and instability. A woman might say her man's name like that in a country at war, but not here. Her face looked so surprised and panicked that he fought the urge to run the other way. Instead, he ran straight back down the hall to see what had snapped under the dreadlocks. He opened the gate, and she fell into his arms with damp eyes.

Her dreads smelled like hair, and Marcus had not smelled hair for a long time. Even the last time he had gotten laid, all he could smell was commercial hair products. She lifted her head with her eyes closed, and Marcus kissed her lips. A slight smell of patchouli entered his consciousness, and he wondered if she had put it on herself, or if it had rubbed off of some hippie guy, but her mouth . . . He had to resist a thought that forced itself on him that he could not go through life without her particular taste. His mind raced. He thought that

Tania must be dealing with some unresolved abandonment issues. That cry for him not to leave sounded so desperate that he couldn't believe it was simply desire. But he decided he was not about to let pop-psychology get in the way. *What is love but a bunch of unresolved issues?* That cry for him not to go had sounded like "please fuck me," and he had been waiting too long to hear that. They held each other tightly as they walked up the stairs, as if in fear of being torn apart. After they got inside, they walked to the bed. She sat down on the bed and unzipped him where he stood, and he got hard in her mouth.

Marcus started getting a little freaked out, though, because she gave a virtuoso performance with her tongue swirling all around him as he felt her stainless steel tongue stud, and as her throat constricted rhythmically. She had obviously learned the tricks on any number of guys, and they irritated him at the same time they delighted. Marcus, despite his general confusion and desire, had serious feelings for her, and didn't want to feel some favorite twist of the tongue favored by a recently deceased tattoo artist. She looked really beautiful down there, but with a kind of beauty few women would understand—a sort of elevating degradation and a physical proof of . . . something . . .

All through this performance, Tania thought of just about nothing. Zip. He pushed her onto the bed and pulled her jeans down to her calves. *"But what if she's HIV positive?"* fell to the onrush of *"How can I get those pants off, quick?"* but her boots laced up to the knee. He couldn't get the jeans over the boots, so he just threw her legs back and fucked her. Tania became very aroused because the pants restrained her around the ankles. If their relationship were to continue, though, she would have to explain to him about how she couldn't come without some form of restraint, but that could wait.

The rubbers sat in the drawer, out of reach, so he "forgot" to use one. After he felt her come the third time, Marcus figured she'd had enough, and as he came in her, the strangest silence washed over him. He heard something like distant pipe organs or choirs, and it was a music he knew he had to get closer to—the music was telling him . . . something.

They lay together enfolded in each others' arms for a long time.

"How do you feel?" asked Tania.

"Better," said Marcus. She giggled and gave him a little slap on the cheek. She raised her face to his, and they kissed. Marcus felt elated, serene, and almost superhuman. Then he said something he never should have said.

"I'll get Snake out for you, Tania."

chapter 13.
THE PASSENGER

*M*ARCUS GOT OUT OF THE DELTA 88 IN FRONT OF THE RUN-DOWN Victorian house with the almost dead tree in front. The house stood on a block lined with similarly run-down shotgun houses. A couple of black teenagers at the end of the block stared at Marcus as he approached the house. Under some sneakers hanging from a phone line, the teenagers sat on BMX-style bicycles made for kids much younger than themselves and wore white T-shirts and pants cut off below the knees. Marcus heard one of them say something the only parts of which he caught were "haunted" and "crazy white boy." He went through the iron gate, which hung slightly open in the center of a spike-topped iron fence. He found himself in a dusty little yard that baked in the glare of a merciless noon.

He looked up when he thought he saw something looking down upon him from the widow's walk, but, when he looked up, he figured it must have been a trick of the light. The knocker created a harsh rap on the door. He waited, then tried again. When he went to look into the window, aluminum foil covered it completely on the inside. Each of the four windows on the porch had the same foil covering.

Just as Marcus started to descend the porch stairs, he heard the door creak open behind him. He turned and saw a thin vertical strip of blackness where the door had opened slightly.

"Hello. I am looking for Necro," said Marcus walking back toward the door slowly. His eyes, accustomed to the glare of midday, could make out nothing inside the blackness.

"That's me," said a voice, rough as if it had not been used for a while.

"I heard you have a hearse. I need one."

"It's not for sale, man."

"Actually, I had only considered renting it for a day or so."

"I don't think so."

"I realize it would be a rather special favor, but it's for Snake."

"What about him?"

"He's passed away."

"I know that. Why are you interrupting my night? Who told you about me?"

"Tomasso, and it's the sort of thing one doesn't talk about on a porch. I'm trying to steal a body. Tomasso said you'd understand."

"Okay, man." The door creaked open far enough to let Marcus in. He entered the darkness and still couldn't make out the figure inside the door. His field of vision glared bright green as his eyes struggled to adjust to the cool darkness of the entrance hall. "What's your problem, man?"

"I am temporarily blind, it seems."

"We're all blind in this life, man. The shapes that move in front of our eyes are just shadows of a world that should have been. We drag our bodies around—hulking masses in league with inertia. Maybe the distant candle of a kiss in our prime flickers in the black distance, but beyond that: darkness. Yeah, we are all blind, man. You know what I mean?"

"Well, usually, but I'm in love at the moment."

"A last leaf in autumn above a brittle carpet of dead leaves—waiting for a skeletal hand to pluck it from a wasted branch. Love. Wake to sleep but take your waking slow, man."

Marcus began to adjust to the darkness. Necro's bug eyes appeared upon a thin and pallid face bordered by long, stringy hair as black as his bell-bottom hip-huggers. An open black shirt revealed a hairless, concave chest and a silver pentagram amulet. He had a low-hanging head, his upper back was curved in a vulpine S, and his hips rested in a thrust forward position. To Marcus, it looked as if he were a gangly corpse used as a necrophiliac giant's string puppet.

"Yes, well, all poetics aside, I need a hearse to carry Snake's body away from the morgue. I should mention that this is highly illegal what we plan to do."

"I know that, man."

"Yes. Quite. Well, I see we understand one another. I can count on your help, then?" Marcus was beginning to make out his surroundings. They seemed to be standing in a long hall with rooms opening out to the right. The outlines of the wide, open doors appeared only because there appeared the faintest hint of candlelight emanating from beyond them. Otherwise, Marcus could see nothing. His hands began to tremble.

"Why are you trying to snatch his body, anyway?" asked Necro. Here Marcus decided to use the approach Tomasso had suggested to try to warm up the clammy Necro to the idea.

"Snake left specific instructions that he wanted to be cremated—you know, the pagan funerary rites of the Vikings and all that—but his sister wants to give him a Christian burial, and has, in fact, legally stolen his corpse in order to force him into a Christian grave."

"They'll never accept the sovereignty of the individual will. How does she know he won't get stuck under the ground for eternity wishing he could get to his place at the long table in

Valhalla and cursing the one that buried him here? I'll go get the key, man, but you can't steal him from the morgue."

"Well, I'm fairly adept at talking my way in and out of many situations, it seems. I don't see why I couldn't."

"Listen, that is, like, the beast down there, man. The morgue thrives on paperwork. You have to jump through some major hoops to get a body out of there. I've tried."

"You have?"

"Yeah. You're not going to the morgue, man. You have to wait and get him out of what they intend for his final resting place. It's no big deal. They don't bury 'em here."

"That is not an option in this case. Snake's being shipped back to the heartland."

"Air freight, or train?"

"I have no idea."

"Come in and have a seat." Necro led the way into one of the doors to the right side of the house. As Marcus entered he saw a single candle sitting upon a skull in the middle of a low round table. By this time his eyes had adjusted enough so that the candle seemed to illuminate the room more than adequately, but this only served to unsettle Marcus further. The ancient marble mantle held at least ten more skulls. The only other furniture in the room, besides the low table, was a pair of chairs facing one another across the table. "Are you disturbed by my artifacts? Most people fall apart when they have to face Truth."

"I . . . I'm . . . Where did you get them?"

"Do you know how many nameless, homeless people die on the streets here every week?"

"No, I suppose not."

"I can usually find three to five bodies a week under the bridge, in abandoned warehouses, under docks . . . murders, alcoholics, drug overdoses, infections, AIDS, drug-resistant strains of tuberculosis, hepatitis. No one cares . . . except me. They're my brothers and sisters, my friends, my associates."

"And how . . ."

"I have techniques."

"Quite."

"You see why I hate the living? You're passing some kind of negative judgment. I can see it on your face. You come to me for help snatching a body, and you dare think I'm crazy? You know there's a church in Eastern Europe that's decorated with bones? They even have chandeliers of human bone— plague victims. You wouldn't pass judgment in that church, but here you think I'm a freak. Let me tell you something. You would have gone straight up to the morgue and got arrested, man, and the penalties are high. Did you know it's even illegal to summon a lousy demon here? There's an actual law on the books. It's the Catholics."

"Quite," said Marcus again.

"Quite. You're nervous, aren't you? Well, fuck you. I'm this close to telling you to get the fuck out of here, man."

Marcus needed Necro. He couldn't let him back out.

"Certainly. I'd be happy to leave. I'm sure the coppers will be happy to hear about your little collection, as well."

"I thought you were cool, man. Now you're not likely to get out of here alive," said Necro, exposing a replica SS dagger.

"It appears we've gotten off on the wrong foot," said Marcus.

"Quite." The skulls in the gloom upon the mantle all of a sudden seemed more real, and Marcus realized that these were the remains of people like him. A grinning, fleshless shell lay just beneath the familiar face he saw each morning in the mirror. Necro's face was lit from below by the candle on the skull in the center of the table as he leaned forward. "I could show you about night," said Necro.

"That won't be necessary. I assure you. I wouldn't report you, really. I was just trying to secure your help. I understand I haven't a proper understanding of your lifestyle . . ."

"This is not a fucking lifestyle. This is the eternal night," said Necro. His eyes bulged.

"I understand," said Marcus not understanding, "but let's put aside our feelings long enough to save Snake from Christian burial." Necro sat back in his chair. He thought.

"The coroner's office'll only release the body to a funeral home—they've got a deal with 'em. So, the body will go to the funeral home before they transport him to wherever it is they want to take him. Funeral homes can be dealt with. That's the weak link. You might not even need a hearse, but we'll take it anyway. What was your name again?"

"Marcus."

"Well, Marcus, try to quit shaking and listen to me. There is nothing strange in my house that you don't already see every day. I think you know. At least you know if you've been in New Orleans long. How long have you been here?"

"Five years in the States. Three years here, approximately."

"Know why you feel so empty after carnival? What's the uneasiness you feel, as if the ground were a sheet of paper that might tear any second leaving a bottomless void under you?" Necro nudged his chin at the mantle. "These are the faces of this city. Nothing living comes from here. What looks like life is only makeup on the cheek of grinning skull—a happy mask looking for a party—drawing the outsider in—and if you outsiders stay too long, the haunting sets in—the decay begins—not being able to drink enough, eat enough, never getting your fill of drugs, sex—whatever. The flesh falls away. The joy falls through your bottomless jaw. I know, man. I know."

"Quite . . ."

"You're quite hopeless. Let's move, then," said Necro, putting the dagger back in its sheath at the small of his back. *Finally*, thought Marcus.

"What are you going to do with the body when we do get him out?" asked Necro.

"I hadn't really settled on what to do with the body. I figured I'd put it in his trailer, hook it up to his car, drive it out to Mississippi, and set it on fire out in the woods."

"That's real class, man," said Necro, smiling and shaking his head.

chapter 14.
THE PARTY

"**D**UDE, WHY DON'T YOU GET OVER YOURSELF?" SAID TANIA INTO Marcus's phone. "You already said you'd fucking dance for three hundred a piece, and I ain't gonna pay you five for shit." On the other end of the connection, the receiver sat wedged between the slender shoulder and the delicate ear of a young stripper. "What's the big difference between dancing on a stage and dancing in a cage?" Tania continued. "You don't even have to get naked!"

Uptown, the skinny blonde twenty-year-old dancer and hooker applied a coat of fire-engine-red nail polish to a pair of hands that had apparently never done dishes.

"That's S&M. It costs extra," she said with a high and vacuous voice.

"Why?" asked Tania indignantly. The dancer hated questions where she had to, like, think about the answer.

"It's extra."

"Listen. Do you want the three hundred, or not? Take it or leave it. It's like two hours work. C'mon." The dancer remained silent for a moment, but Tania's voice sounded abusive and commanding, so she began to warm up to her.

"Yeah. Okay. Will you be there? You have to pay me up front."

"You'll get your fuckin' money."

"Okay. Okay I guess."

"Fuckin' right it's okay. Just like it was okay when you made the deal last week. Don't fuck with me any more! Be there at five!" Tania hung up.

All of these arrangements and phone calls had begun to bring Tania down because she had to trust a bunch of flakes for every aspect of the coming party, a party for which she bore the entire responsibility and which would begin in only four hours. She needed to leave for the old school shortly, where the party would soon commence, and had resolved very little with all the people who had promised to help. The old school had never been wired with a phone, so she would not be able to communicate with anyone after she arrived. She pressed the record button on Marcus's answering machine, and said, "Listen up. I'm down at the party, 496 Bucelle Street, and they don't have a phone down there. Everybody just stop asking questions and giving me attitude. Just bring your ass and everything you need, and get down there to set up, and don't wait till the last minute. If you want to leave a message for Big Marc, do it at the beep."

As she walked to the bathroom to put some glitter on her eyelids, she muttered, "I've got to get out of this town. Nobody's got their shit together." She wore a black taffeta, strapless evening gown, which she had recently bought from a thrift store for $50. It left her entire snake tattoo, from hand to hand, head to tail, exposed for viewing. The elegance of the gown complimented the earthiness of her dreads. She looked in the mirror, still dissatisfied, and applied glitter viciously. She had a distracted look on her face. There she stood, finally complete. Even the dreads had been freshly dyed. Yet she didn't experience the fulfillment she had expected to come from her completion. Instead, she felt empty and spent, having literally nothing to do with the rest of her life as she saw it. She did look forward to traveling, but that just seemed like normal living to her. As far as actual goals, she had none. Another tattoo, maybe, she half thought, and then she asked herself if she was kidding.

On top of this empty feeling, the party had strained her composure. Her jitters had gotten pretty bad from the morning coffee that usually steadied her nerves, and Tania needed some support. She walked back to the bed, and lay face down on it. Munchy got up from where he lay at the foot of the bed and licked her feet. She let him. Her face buried in a pillow, she inhaled Marcus's scent. *Oh, I'm so fucking nuts. Dude, how could you have let him go steal Snake's body? He might end up in jail or hurt or something. He's sweet. I wish . . . Oh, fuck dude, you're getting retarded. Shut up.*

She rolled over, picked up the phone, and called a cab. Munchy became hyper-alert as she went to the refrigerator and pulled out a raw pot roast. "Okay, sit." Munchy sat. "I'm going to leave you here all night alone cause I don't want you killing any guests. This is just to make up for it in advance, sweety." She dropped the pot roast. Munchy grabbed it out of the air and started chewing it like a piece of bubble gum. From the coat hook near the door, she removed the silky black shawl with the long fringe, and put it over her shoulders to keep the tattoo under wraps as she left.

Fifteen minutes later, as the taxi pulled away, she stood baking in the sun in the front of the tall gate to the old Saint Mary Magdalene Catholic Girl School. The school stood three stories high with its horseshoe floor plan enclosing, on three sides, a playground of small weeds, dust, and cracked concrete that was separated from the street by a spiked iron fence.

"Hey, Tania. I'm almost done," shouted Herman from a window on the third floor, his goat beard wagging in the wind as he finished up some final spot welds on a cage that hung down from the third-floor window and left an entrance to the cage through a window on the second floor. A similar cage hung directly across the playground on the other wing of the school.

"Where's Tomasso?" Tania shouted back. "He's supposed to be set up by now."

"Haven't seen him."

"Dude, are you the only one here?"

"Julie's around somewhere."

"Great." Tania entered the dusty playground and looked around at the emptiness and the three floors of windows with most of the panes broken out. "Fuck." She reached into her black leather purse, pulled out a flask of liquor, and took a swig—then another, and another. In her evening gown, she was a truly bizarre apparition as she walked to the center of the deserted playground. She took another swig. "Where is everybody?" Tania had always been there for the show, wherever "there" meant or whatever "the show" happened to be, but she had never actually put on any kind of show. She had never actually organized something of the kind she loved to attend. In contrast to the amazing feeling of togetherness and communion she felt at great music shows or parties or raves, she now felt—not loneliness. Aloneness seemed a more appropriate word.

The feeling didn't shake off, either; it seemed to force itself with great strength upon her along with an unwanted realization—unwanted like her first period, or like the time she had actually faced the full force of the fact that her mother was never coming back home. Her arms hung at her sides, and her head tilted listlessly as she stood in the center of the deserted playground.

This space was the light that had shone through from beyond the images that had possessed her for so long, as if she had finally become the slide in the slide viewer and lay facing the bare light—a light her existence would now tint for others, but an illusion she worried she could never share again. From then on, she knew everything she did would have to have some substance to it. Either that or she would have to find another dream to pursue, and she didn't feel up to it. Tania was tired. She stood almost catatonic, as if stripped of her home, family, and country—as if she would have stood there until someone told her to move, or until the universe ended, whichever came first. She stared at the dust. The dream of the tattoo was dying—a dream that she had grown into so fully it had turned into a skin—a skin that having served its purpose began to shed—and underneath the peeling layer a shiny, alien surface began to emerge. *I guess I'm a woman now. Fuck. Fuck! I guess this means I won't like MTV or 90210 anymore, either*, she said to herself disgustedly.

"Are you okay?" asked Julie, who had come from inside the school.

"Dude, I'm kind of burnt out," said Tania not turning around to face Julie, the architect who rented the school from the archdiocese and lived in it in a fine style. She lived only on the third floor in the midst of a collection of found objects—booths from old Denny's restaurants, the guts of pianos, parts of engines painted bright colors, an old bar upholstered in black vinyl, the old throne of a toilet with a glass top used for a coffee table, a huge fiberglass jester's head from an old Mardi Gras float up in the corner, a single twin bed in the center of the room with a red velvet bedspread, and curtains made from a bolt of gold lame fabric she had found down by the wharves one night—at least she told everyone that she found it. She looked a bit frowzy like her collections, with her long, bleached hair streaked with black, orange, and fuchsia, and showing inch-long, dark roots. She wore a thin, stretchy black turtleneck worn out over a pair of men's gabardine slacks—spooky eyes, too.

"Why don't you come upstairs and lie down for a little while," she said.

"Yeah," said Tania taking two more gulps from her bottle, killing it, "Okay. You got any liquor up there?"

"Sure, babe."

Tania had a few more drinks upstairs, passed out, and *fuck the party.*

chapter 15.
SNOWBALL'S CHANCE IN HELL

MARCUS, BEHIND THE WHEEL OF THE HEARSE, AND NECRO, IN THE passenger seat, eyed the other hearse that held Snake's body and idled near the back door of a funeral home in a run-down neighborhood of plank houses. They had followed the other hearse there from the morgue, and the driver still sat in the driver's seat smoking a cigarette.

"Let's see if we get a break here. If we do, it'll save us a lot of trouble," said Necro, his eyes completely invisible behind a pair of huge dark glasses—the total UV-coverage ones so popular with retirees. After a few minutes, the driver of the hearse that bore Snake opened his door and walked inside the wooden funeral home, which had a patina of peeling white paint. "Bingo," said Necro. "Pull up."

Marcus pulled the gurgling old Cadillac hearse up next to the newer one. Necro jumped out and tried the back door of the other hearse. It was open, and Necro disappeared into the back. He reemerged, giving a thumbs-up. According to plan, Marcus got out of the hearse and trotted over to meet Necro. Snake was not in a casket yet. He lay in a body bag. Necro flipped over the body bag, and pushed it as Marcus squatted and began to maneuver it onto his shoulder.

"What dat is?" asked a husky seven-year-old, who jogged up wearing only a pair of acid-washed jeans cut off at the knees.

"Nothing, son. Run along," said Marcus as they loaded the corpse onto his shoulder.

"Dat be a dead man, yay . . . Bobo!" barked the kid. Another kid, this one skinny, ran up wearing the same uniform. "Dat be a dead man, Bobo." Bobo removed his thumb from his mouth.

"Unh-unh. You be trippin', Dookie." Dookie hit Bobo in the chest. Bobo stepped back and planted his thumb back in his mouth. Marcus stood, and, with Snake draped over his shoulder, began to walk quickly to the back of the old Caddilac hearse. Dookie grabbed his pants leg, slowing him down.

"Why you be stealin' a dead man?" asked Dookie, with Bobo close behind him.

"We aren't stealing a dead man. Let go of my pants!" hissed Marcus.

"Den what choo be doin' wid 'im?" Necro ran up and grabbed Dookie by the shoulder, shaking him.

"You better get the fuck away from here, kid," said Necro.

"Ow! Le' go! Tashanda!" yelled Dookie. An eleven-year-old girl in a pink T-shirt dress and pink plastic-beaded pigtails ran from across the street followed by a younger girl.

"You bettah put yo hands off my nephew, motherfucker!"

"You little fuckers better get away from here!" said Necro, releasing Dookie. Marcus had broken free, and with his free hand he opened the back of the hearse. He placed Snake next to the other body bag, which held a spare body that Necro had kept cooling in his walk-in refrigerator. The body felt chilly against his shoulder as he loaded it on. It took him half a minute, and when he reemerged from behind the hearse carrying the bagged body, he saw that a small crowd of children had now gathered.

"I'm a go tell dat man you be stealin' dat dead man," said Tashanda. "Don' be thinkin' you can run, no. I screams loud.

Wanna hear?" Tashanda opened her mouth wide and clamped her eyes closed.

"No!" said Marcus.

"You want me to shut up, I gotta get paid. 'Stan' what I'm sayin'?" said Tashanda. Marcus lay the body down in the new hearse, and reached into his back pocket. The kids all took a quick couple of steps backward, then relaxed again when they saw the wallet come out. He fished out a five and handed it to her.

"Chump change!" said Dookie.

"Yay. I need me a hundred!"

"All I have in cash is five more," said Marcus, eyes darting toward the back door to the funeral parlor. They had to get out quick.

"Fuck!" said Dookie. "Give it heah, but you gots to take us down to Cool Breeze."

"What?"

"Dat snowball stand by Claiborne," said Tashanda. "We gots to get snowballs."

"If we take you, will you shut the fuck up? I don't want to meet any cops," said Necro, now taking a conciliatory tone.

"Fuck a police! My uncle what choo gots to worry bout! . . . puttin' yo' white hands on dat black baby. He fuck yo' ass up."

"You got to ride in the back, though. You still want to go?"

"Yay," said Tashanda and Dookie in unison.

"But you gots to pay me dat five," said Tashanda.

"Okay," said Marcus, handing her the bill, "but just you three. None of the other kids."

"Arigh,'" said Tashanda.

The New Orleans summer felt like baked steam and dust particles served over pavement. The temperature that day was 96 degrees in the shade, and the hearse, though dark, had no opening windows or air conditioning. Only a small window let the light in at the back. Marcus moved Snake to the extreme left side of the hearse, and sat himself down at the other extreme. So did Tashanda and Bobo. They eyed the body bag nervously, but Dookie sat right down on Snake's chest.

"I'm a get grape . . . large," he said.

"Grape? Grape is punk," said Tashanda.

"Unh-unh!" said Bobo.

"What choo be gettin'?" Dookie asked Tashanda.

"Nectar." The kids had dreamy looks on their faces as they discussed flavors for the rest of the eight-minute ride. When the doors finally opened, Marcus was soaked with sweat and feeling dizzy. He stood panting in the sun. Then Dookie grabbed his pant leg again.

"C'mon, mistuh!"

"We brought you here, now we have to go," said Marcus.

"How we gonna walk back from heah?" asked Tashanda.

"We don't have time to chauffeur you kids around." Tashanda took a deep breath, opened her mouth wide, and clamped her eyes again. Marcus conceded. They walked to the window of a little whitewashed shack on four-lane Claiborne Avenue. The snowball stand adjoined a bar with tinted windows on one side, and on the other a chicken shack. In the vicinity stood cubic hotels that rented rooms by the hour, vacant lots, a neutral ground full of tall weeds, a gas station, and a brick housing project with some tall oak trees in the courtyard. The whole scene seemed sculpted out of varying densities of dust. The young woman inside the window eyed Marcus suspiciously, but went to make the snowballs. They heard the grinding sound come out of the shack as she prepared the ice. The snowballs each came out of the window in a Styrofoam cup, with a straw and a spoon stuck in the half sphere of brightly-colored shaved ice visible above the rim.

"Hey Mistuh," said Dookie holding up a large, red snow-ball. "I got choo strawberry." Marcus dug the pink spoon into the red ice, and shoveled the soft snow into his mouth where it melted into sensations of tart, sweet, wet. It tasted more like a big cold strawberry than a strawberry ever did, and had no nutritional value whatsoever.

"Thanks, Dookie," said Marcus. They stood there eating and drinking their snowballs until their tongues had all turned the colors of their flavors. After they had cooled off, Tashanda said, "Let's get the fuck outa heah fo' my mamma fine out."

They arranged themselves as before in the hearse, but now, as the heat climbed again, the snowballs cooled them. Dookie let some of his spill onto Snake's body bag as he worked hard on his snowball.

"Sweet," said Dookie.

"Sweet," said Marcus.

chapter 16.
THE BODY SNATCHERS

AFTER THEY HAD DROPPED THE KIDS OFF, MARCUS AND NECRO drove away toward Snake's trailor.

"That was a fiasco, man. What a bunch of little sons of bitches," said Necro.

"They turned out to be rather likeable," said Marcus, "the little weeds."

"You can tell they've seen a few body bags before, man."

"Well, it's actually done now. I don't know what to say. Thank you, Necro. I owe you an eternal debt of gratitude. You did make sure that was Snake, didn't you."

"Of course."

"Listen. You really should attend the funeral party in the Bywater. I'll be back from Mississippi in about three hours, so maybe I can run into you down there."

"I suppose I could stand a party. I need to be getting out of the house more. I'll try to get down there after sunset. I despise being out in the daytime like this."

"I understand . . . eternal night," said Marcus.

Twenty minutes later they pulled up at Snake's trailer, and went to the door. Marcus put the key in the lock, and the lock wouldn't turn.

"Bollocks! She changed the bloody locks!"

"We might be able to break in." Necro walked around to the trailer hitch. "It looks like you've got a bigger problem here, man. He's got an attachment of, like, two-inch-thick steel welded around this hitch." Marcus came running, and saw the hitch had a roughly welded steel attachment wrapped around it and welded to a steel post embedded in the ground. "Your portable immolation chamber isn't so portable any-more, man. You better stick him in the trunk of his car, and work from there."

"Good thinking." Marcus dashed to the back of the orange Roadrunner and opened the trunk. "Bollocks! What the hell is this junk?"

Necro came up behind him.

"Man, just relax a minute. He's got this thing set up for racing. That's a kick-ass fuel system," said Necro, looking at the fuel lines and boxes that took up the trunk area. "Try the back seat." Marcus ran to the door. Steel reinforcements kept the seats from moving.

"Bloody bloody hell!"

"Yeah. The whole driver's cage is steel reinforced. Looks like Snake was pretty handy with a welding torch." Marcus's whole world seemed to collapse around him. He jumped in the front seat and tried the ignition, but the key didn't work.

"Bloody thorough woman, isn't she?" said Marcus.

"I can hot-wire that. No problem. Your problem is getting him into the car." After a quick examination of the situation, it became apparent that they couldn't possibly fit Snake in the back because of the steel reinforcements. Necro got into the driver's side.

"Look, man. We've got to cut him up so you can fit him on the floor of the front seat. The body bag won't leak, so don't worry about it." Necro handed Marcus the replica SS dagger, then turned to work on the hot-wire under the dash.

"Are you mad? I mean . . . are you bloody mad?"

"You are starting to get on my nerves again, man," said Necro as he pulled at a wire. "I don't like it when you make these uninformed value judgments."

"Uninformed? No. You've just informed me that you want to hack Snake into bits. I hardly think I'm uninformed. You are bloody mad!"

"All right, maybe I'm crazy enough to drag Snake out on the ground and leave you here to deal with him. Would you like that, man?"

"No. We're going to put him in your ghastly refrigerator, and resolve this at a more leisurely pace. It's the only sensible thing to do."

"You can't put that body in my refrigerator. He's hot."

"What do you mean 'he's hot'? You can't get much colder than old Snake at this moment."

"I only save bodies that nobody cares about. It's a rule, and it keeps me out of trouble. You have to cut him up, and get him out of my hearse right fucking now, man, 'cause I'm sick of your shit. It's no big deal. Just think of it as steak," said Necro as the thunderous engine started.

"Okay. Wait. Let me think. Let's just put him in the front seat of the car. Nobody will notice he's dead. He'll just look stoned."

"That's a bad idea, man." Necro pulled himself out from under the steering wheel and dashboard. "He can keep a poker face, but if a cop pulls up beside you, you'll panic. I can tell."

"Look, you. Just help me." Marcus walked over to the hearse, opened up the back doors, got into the back, and unzipped the bag. What he saw was not shocking just because it was the dead body of someone he had known, but because he was naked. "He's nude!" exclaimed Marcus.

"Quite," said Necro, "what did you expect, man, a tux? He's got a hard-on, too. That's Snake all right."

"Oh, my God!"

"I bet that's what all the girls used to say." Indeed, the member stood there like a pale gray daikon.

"Do you have any clothing in that hearse?" asked Marcus.

"No way, man."

Marcus looked around and spied a clothesline a few trailers down. He dashed to it, and grabbed an XXXL T-shirt sporting a pointing horizontal finger and the legend "I'M WITH STUPID." He dashed back to the hearse, jumped in the back, and worked the T-shirt onto Snake as Necro watched from outside. He managed to get it over Snake's head, but getting his arms through the sleeves was out of the question. Snake didn't seem that terribly stiff, but he certainly wasn't flexible.

"Let's move him," said Marcus, as he jumped out of the back and pulled Snake by the feet toward the outside. Necro grabbed Snake under the arms. They stood him up against the back fender of the Roadrunner and opened the pas- senger door, which Snake had apparently not gotten around to welding shut. The "I'M WITH STUPID" shirt came down to Snake's mid thigh and tented out at the crotch about ten inches. Snake's heels left trails in the dust as they dragged him to the door and finally pushed him in. They managed to get him bent enough to seat him in what would appear a natural position to a quick glance, but his eyes still stared glazed-over in a milky white. Marcus snatched the shades off of Necro's face.

"Ow," said Necro, temporarily blinded by the merciless sunlight. "Gimme back my glasses, man."

"I'll bring them back in a few days."

Necro considered taking them back or waiting for Marcus to return them later. He decided he didn't want to fight over them if it would get him away from Marcus quicker.

"Okay. Just keep 'em. He's your problem now, man. Wish I could say it's been a pleasure."

"This has not been a lark for me either," snapped Marcus, turning away from Snake only to see Necro already walking away toward the hearse. As the engine rumbled, Marcus went right back to work trying to make Snake look natural. He tried to close his jaw by pushing up on it, but it fell right back down. Necro's hearse kicked up a little haze of dust as it passed. Closing the door of the car and stepping back, Marcus looked at Snake through the window and realized the improbability of any casual observer getting suspicious over the way he looked. At any rate, it would have to do.

Once in the driver's seat of the Roadrunner, Marcus realized that even though Snake had been refrigerated for two days, a very bad odor had started to emanate from him. With morbid fascination, Marcus watched a drop of condensation roll down Snake's gray face. *It's OK. It's okay. They'll just think it's sweat*, thought Marcus as he put the car in gear and applied a little pressure to the gas pedal, which threw him across the drive and caused the back tire to spin and throw up a cloud of dust. "Christ!" On the next try, he began to get some control of the car, and rolled toward the entrance to the trailer park. But the first lunge of the car had sent him so far that another car entering the trailer park went by heading in the opposite direction on his right side. Marcus felt relieved that he had finished with the business of loading the body into the car as quickly as he did, even though the whole process after removing Snake from the hearse had only taken about a minute and a half. He realized how dangerous what he had done had been, and how close he had come to having a car roll right by as they carried a corpse with a large hard-on pointing at the sky like a flagpole without a country.

Elizabeth felt a little differently as she drove past the Roadrunner to her right and saw her brother's yawning face through the window. Her scream was muffled by the insulated interior of her white 1992 Lumina, as she grabbed for her car phone and hit "911". As he left the trailer park, Marcus didn't notice her car turning around in a tight circle to follow. Elizabeth's face contorted with righteous Midwestern indignation as only the face of a crossed woman who is used to getting her way can.

chapter 17.
CUTTING TO THE CHASE

WHAT DID ELIZABETH LOOK LIKE? I COULD DESCRIBE HER, BUT SHE was such an asshole when I called her that I would rather not spend any time on her. She did some things that figure into the outcome, but you wouldn't want to know her, so I'm not going to describe her for you. You're on your own. Imagine her any way you want. A Giraffe. A cloud of steam. A wad of toilet paper. An opossum. Well, she actually did remind me of an opossum. Fine. Think of her as an opossum wearing a shoulder-padded WalMart blouse and cheapo makeup.

"Someone stole one of my cars!" yelled Elizabeth into the phone, realizing she had better ease the police into the story so they wouldn't think she was unbalanced. "They're heading toward the city on Airline Highway. I'm in my car following. I'm in a white Lumina, and the stolen car is an old orange sports car with a skull painted on the roof . . . Okay. Wait just a moment. It's coming up . . . Okay. Cross street Michard Avenue. Hurry! Okay. I'm not hanging up."

Marcus drove as conservatively as he could, considering the car he drove. At every light on the highway, he would pull into the far right lane to avoid anyone staring at Snake for too long. Just idling, the huge hemi engine made the car shudder, and it was loud as hell. In the distance, above the dusty glare, gas stations, and fast food restaurants that lined the thoroughfare, loomed the Causeway Overpass from which he intended to take the short jog over to Interstate 10 and from there head to Mississippi.

"Snake, old man, we're on the way now. Nothing like a nice drive. Not that I'm calling your last wishes into question, mind you, but if I ever write a will, I'll make it very simple—very simple indeed. Just 'I, Marcus Crowley, being of sound mind and body, leave all my earthly possessions to X. Please dispose of my body in the most expedient fashion available'—no profane last statements, no dancing girls, no deejays, no necrotic erections, no—no nothing. I'll die with a little dignity—not that I'm casting any aspersions on your blasted, tacky will, you bastard."

A police car hooked in behind him, and turned its flashing blue lights and siren on. Three quarters of a cup of pure adrenaline dumped into Marcus's bloodstream—so much that he could taste it bitter on his tongue and smell it through his nasal membranes. His heart nearly stopped and then began beating in time with the engine as he fought off the imperatives his body was sending him to release various bodily fluids. Marcus pulled over to the side and stopped.

"Turn off your engine, and step away from the car with your hands behind your head!" blared the loudspeaker on the police car. Marcus's hands shook violently. "Turn off your engine now!"

Marcus jammed the gas pedal into the seventh dimension.

"Bloody. Bloody. Bloody fucking hell," said Marcus. The Roadrunner's hemi engine screamed bloody murder and the blurred Mickey T. big meat tires sprayed the police car with a shower of gravel. Marcus noticed the engine was winding up and his speed was not increasing, probably because he had not downshifted when he had slowed to a stop. Through the windshield, he noticed that the hood tach was redlining above 6000. He eased off the gas, and the tires finally gained traction. His head slammed back against the headrest, and the broken dividing lines on the pavement turned instantaneously into a single solid white stripe. He started shifting, and the speedometer needle immediately pointed to 150. He managed to make it past an intersection just after the light had turned red. Another intersection approached, and Marcus applied some heavy brake to slow down enough to make the right turn. His tires squealed as he cut the wheel and headed for River Road.

The cops had gotten blocked by a line of cars and trucks crossing in front of them, and so had lost sight of Marcus in the split-second business of chasing a beast like the Roadrunner.

The rise upon which the train tracks rode sent Marcus into the air as he crossed over it, but on the other side he found himself on smooth streets in a residential neighborhood.

Slowing down, he tried to catch his breath and his thoughts, and missed both. Up ahead he could see where the road stopped at the beginning of the green uphill grade of the levee, a tall earthwork that ran along the riverbank to keep the Mississippi in its bed. Over the top of the levee, he could see the tops of tall trees, and in front of it ran River Road. *I'll never get out of this!* As he stopped at the intersection of River Road, Marcus made a quick decision. When he found a break in the traffic, he crossed River Road, jumped the curb, and drove up the mown turf of the levee to the crest.

The levee seemed twice as steep on the other side, but he decided he could drive along and use it for cover without tipping over if he took it slow. All he could see on his right was grass, and to his left, the sky. Snake's head leaned against the window. After driving about two hundred yards Marcus stopped the car, got out, and walked on all fours up to the crest of the levee. Peering over the apex of the earthen wall, he heard a few sirens, and then saw two police cars tearing down River Road, passing his position. Another came out of the neighborhood, drove a block, and turned back in, disappearing again. This scene repeated itself several times over the next few minutes. Eventually the searching seemed to stop.

Marcus had to assume a more relaxed-looking position because of people walking their dogs along the top of the levee. A couple on horseback even greeted him. He sat for hours cross-legged near the top of the levee on the mown grass, in a paralysis of anxiety. His only real problem arose when kids on bicycles insisted upon asking him about his cool car. "My friend is sick," he'd say. "Don't go down there and bother him, okay?" That seemed to keep them away. As the sun grew low, he walked down to the car and got back in. Snake was a bit more ghastly looking, and the odor had become a real problem, but Marcus told himself it would all be over in an hour or so. As he touched the two bare ignition wires together, they sparked and started the engine again with a growl but Marcus noticed that the gasoline gauge needle pointed to E.

After he drove down the levee, he reentered the quiet neighborhoods of suburban Jefferson Parish, navigating the streets carefully and stopping at the corners to make sure no police waited on the cross streets. In front of one of the houses, he saw a Wormwood Spring Water delivery truck with its side panel up exposing a wall of plastic five-gallon jugs. The delivery man had just entered the house carrying two full bottles of spring water, one on his shoulder, the other grasped by the neck at his side. Marcus pulled up, got out, quickly removed one of the empties, and drove on. When he got back on Airline Highway, he headed straight for the first gas station he came across. When he went inside to pay, he bought a pair of cheap panty hose to use as a mask in case he had to run from the cops again. He also bought a gallon jug of water. Outside, he dumped out the water from the gallon jug and filled it with gasoline. He also filled the five-gallon jug with gasoline, then filled the car up. He placed the full five-gallon jug of gas between Snake's legs, and put the gallon jug by his side. He froze when he saw a police car go by, but the cop hadn't been paying attention and didn't notice the orange Mopar. Considering his options, Marcus drove out onto Airline Highway again, then pulled up at an industrial building. He drove around the back, and parked behind a dumpster. There he breathed gasoline fumes until after sunset.

Finally he got his nerve up, started the car, and managed to get onto the ramp at Causeway Boulevard. From there he made it to the interstate and headed in the direction of Mississippi. Everything seemed peaceful out on the highway, and the car hummed under a sky that glowed orange from reflected mercury vapor lights. The interstate took him past downtown New Orleans, and as he took the high, long curve that passed the downtown area at about 40 feet off the ground, it felt as if the car had wings. For some reason, the place looked stunningly beautiful—the Superdome, Charity Hospital, all the diverse architectural styles downtown. The intensity of the senseless past few weeks seemed to bear down upon him with their full weight, and tears streamed down his cheeks.

Marcus had to bend the only ear he could.

"Snake. I'm alive, and I don't even care if I die right now. Is that how you felt? That's why you were always on, isn't it? You lived every day like this, didn't you? No time for the bollocks, eh?" Snake in profile looked like a monk droning silently against the dusk and the dark buildings. "Well, bugger, Snake, I'm with you! In an hour I'm going to set you ablaze in the piney woods of Mississippi with nobody there to see it. And get to see some stars for a change. I'll hitch back and listen to bloody . . . fucking . . . whatever. Tammy Wynette! In the cab of a big rig, God damn it, and listen to the driver talk about . . . I don't know . . . truckstop girls or something. In a southern accent! If it took all this drama to wake me up, so be it, because this is sheer poetry—our poetry. We're brothers, Snake, you and me."

However, Snake had never really been reflective when he was alive. The closest he ever got to poetry was listening to Nine Inch Nails singing *I want to fuck you like an animal* or when someone wanted an old-style tattoo that said "~America~ Love it or leave it." Even then he didn't really like to do lettering. His life would be poetry only in the hands of a poet. His life was not poetry. Poets write poetry. His life was his life. He lived it. Marcus had no brother. He could have a woman, maybe, and that was his only narrow ledge on the infinite cliff face of existence. Marcus was Marcus. Snake was Snake. A police car came up the on-ramp, spotted the Roadrunner, and turned on its spectral blue lights, sending Marcus into higher flights of poetic bliss or making him panic or both or neither or whatever etcetera.

chapter 18.
SPEECHLESS IN BYWATER

"**L**OOK, I TOLD YOU I'M NOT PAYIN' YOUR ASS EXTRA," SAID TANIA to the stripper in the Catholic schoolgirl outfit. From inside the second floor of the school, the stripper eyed the window she would have to crawl through to enter the cage.

"I just don't want to get in there. It's not safe," said the stripper in a whine that always seemed to work on guys. Tania, however, didn't play that.

"Herman knows how to weld. Don't gimme that. You know the moving sculpture in the Albanian plaza? That's Herman's. Don't tell me he can't build a sturdy cage." Herman, who stood nearby with Julie, looked a little irritated.

"I've been working inside that cage all day. It's really safe."

"Working is not dancing," said the hooker.

"You want dancing?" asked a disgusted Tania. She climbed through the window into the cage and started to jump up and down. "Here's the pogo!" Then she began to bounce against the bars. "The slam!" she cried as she bashed, then climbed back through the window again, and said "Now that's dancing—not that little gyro thing you do."

"Well, like—okay," said the dancer.

"Fine!" Tania turned on her heel and walked toward the exit of the empty classroom in the gathering gloom. The sun had sunk low in the sky, leaving only an orange glow.

Tomasso had shown up with his Jaguar stuffed with PA equipment. He had set up a table with his CD players, mixers, and turntable at the front window on the second floor. One window away, Ned, a bald, fiftyish man in a conservative blazer who did sound and lighting at a local club, had set up his power amps and lighting mixers. Tania had begged him to get a follow-spot, but all he had managed to get hold of were some can lights and gels. Just below Tomasso's and Ned's position stood Marilyn at the top of the steps to the main entrance, saying "Check. Testing. Testing." in a seductive voice into the mic atop a stand. The PA screeched feedback.

"Ned. Please," Marilyn yelled up to the window.

"Okay," said Ned, "I think it ought to work now."

"Check. Testing. Testing," said Marilyn. The PA screeched again.

Behind her, near the door, a kid with cut-off shorts, no shirt, and a jester's hat aimed a stream of water from a hose into an old claw-footed bathtub. Tomasso pressed the play button on a CD player, and the Chemical Brothers slammed out of the loudspeakers, which he had placed in the windows on both sides of the school. Two tattooed women in old party dresses had set up a bar in one of the ground floor windows to the left side of the school, and already the guests had begun to trickle in through the front gate.

By the time night fell, the playground and the ground floor of the school had filled with people who drank cocktails out of plastic cups and milled. A cadre of dreadlocked freaks hung out on the outside of the fence and acted "tribal" by lighting whatever newspapers lay on the street and dancing around the fires like a convention of village idiots. Doctor Indiri actually showed up in answer to Tania's invitation, rode his Harley through the front gate, and parked it with the other bikes: BSA, Norton, Triumph, Moto Guzzi,

Laverda, and BMW—no rice-rockets. Necro walked from
one bike to the next admiring and studying them. Balding
men wore what hair they had left on their heads and chins
cropped to crew-cut length with black sport coats over black
T-shirts above shiny silver belt buckles. They had left their
aspirations to be art dealers and media moguls on the other
side of Esplanade Avenue, and showed off their immacu-
lately lipsticked dates, who were striking dour-faced poses.
Serious artists held frivolous conversations, laughed, talked
painting, derided or praised other serious artists, and drank
and drank and drank. Good poets stooped to bad poetry and
excess verbiage to impress generous women like good-
natured little flowers in their blue, orange, or purple vintage
dresses from '50s and '60s suburbia. Prats who looked like
they had hired Tom Waits as a fashion consultant struck
even worse poses than the wannabe art dealers and media
moguls' girlfriends, and attracted the most confused of the
women with good fashion sense. A sexually magnetic 19-
year-old had an excuse to pull up her dress and expose her
ass to show off one of Snake's tattoos. A circle of guys pretended to appreciate the artistry as they marveled at the full-
ness of her white bottom. Vampire types scowled from the
dark corners and passages, and a seven-foot Rastafarian in a
green sharkskin suit and dark sunglasses spoke in deep tones
to an emaciated model. A summit of tattooed bartenders
from the most eccentric bars in town convened near the
bathroom door.

After the guy with no shirt and a jester's hat dumped several buckets of dry ice into the bathtub at the top of the
steps, a thick fog began to run down the steps like a water-
fall to fill the playground in the still evening air. The fog
obscured the Airwalk sneakers, the sea-foam green stiletto
heels, the work boots, the Beatle boots, the Doc Martens of

every style: greasy black, distressed leather, chemically treated, shiny, peacock blue, red, green, oxblood, low-topped boot, high-topped boot, and even sandal.

Inside the school, leaning on a first-floor window ledge, Sarge surveyed the crowd. By his sides stood Red Rover and Snake, also surveying the crowd.

"This place is extremely vulnerable to attack," said Sarge, "I think the only way to defend it is to each take a position on one face of the building, and set up a crossfire. Red, I want you to go wire some claymores along the perimeter."

"Sure, Sarge," said Red Rover with his vaporous hair floating in a nonexistent breeze. "I'll get on that pretty soon." Sarge watched as the two ghosts ignored him.

"Tania's all right. Look at this shit," said Snake looking better to Sarge than he had when he was alive. "I didn't think she could pull it off. I guess she never had trouble pulling it off before. Know what I mean?" Snake tried to elbow Sarge, but his elbow went right through him.

"Snake, you're such a moron," said Red Rover. "When you die, it's supposed to, like, wake you up."

"Fuck it, man. I'm just as retarded as I ever was. I've been using my invisibility to like look up girls' skirts n' shit. You ought to try it."

"That doesn't sound like what you're supposed to be doing, man. It's kind of disrespectful. Aren't you worried you might catch Hell in the next life?"

"What do you mean, 'the next life'?"

"Yeah," said Red Rover, "Ghosts only get three—maybe four hundred years."

"That sucks."

Bill Relf, Prytania's father, passed by the front of the school in his navy-blue LeBaron. Tania's message on his answering machine had said that this party was a big moment for her, and she wanted him to be there. He looked at the scene, scowled, and drove on.

AUTHOR: So, why couldn't you be there for your daughter?

WILLIAM RELF: Wait. Who the hell are you to take that tone with me? You don't know anything. You understand that? You don't know what I've gone through for her, but she always manages to make anything I do for her blow up in my face. It's a good thing I didn't stick around or that would have blown up in my face, too. I could see it coming. That's why I left. Plus I dislike being in such close proximity to a bunch of druggie punks like you.

A: Let's not get personal.

WR: Look at yourself. Needle marks. Skinny. Out of shape. You live in a dump. No respect. Do your parents know what you're doing to yourself?

A: I'm beginning to see why Mrs. Relf left you.

WR: She left because she was a poster child for the Me Generation. Listen, I know what you're doing here. First you infer that somehow I don't care about my daughter, and then you try to infer that her mother leaving was my fault. How could you put that crap in your arm and then give me a lecture on giving a shit about anything? I know your type. It's just blame the guy with the suit for everything. I spent my life breaking my neck trying to provide for my family and hold things together, and then I gotta listen to some flake try to make it sound like it's my fault it all fell apart. Okay, maybe it is my fault. Maybe I could learn something from you. Got any drugs? We could sit around here and get high in your cool warehouse, man.

A: I'm not trying to say . . .

WR: It's just blame the guy with the suit. Blame the guy with the suit. Listen, freak, you aren't shit to me, either.

A: I'm not shit to anybody, man. I'm a poster child for the worst generation.

Tania stood inside the school with her back to the front door, through which guests sporadically passed in order to find the bathroom. She and Julie complimented each other's hair and clothing.

"Hi, Tania," said a voice from behind her. She turned, and there stood Manny and Paulo. Tania's heart jumped, and she took three quick steps backward. "Don't worry Tania. Apologize to Tania, Paulo."

"It was just business," said Paulo. "Don't take it personal. I just went nuts."

"I said *apologize!*" barked Manny.

"I am very sorry, Tania."

Tania just stood there with her heart pounding.

"It's really okay, Tania," said Manny. "I've explained the whole situation to him, and how he has to behave. He grew up in a totally different way. You can't imagine. He really has no desire to hurt anyone. You know, he always thinks what he does is self-defense."

"Yeah," said Paulo. "I know you just got all mixed up in this shit, and I feel bad 'cause you one of Manny's good friends, an' listen, if you ever need a favor, I know I owe you, so you just call Paulo, and I make yo problem disappear."

"That's all right," said Tania, knees wobbling.

"Well, we're going to mill a little, and see and be seen," said Manny. "Fabulous party."

"Cool," said Tania, as they disappeared into the crowd. She took a deep breath.

When the time came to start the program, Tania sought out Marilyn and found her in the ladies' room.

"Oh! I just love the lashes! How do you get 'em to do that?" asked Tania, flattering the best way she knew.

"Oh, honey. That's a trade secret."

"I really love your look. It's so fake looking." Marilyn stopped working on her lashes and stared at Tania in the mirror. "I mean . . . that's a compliment. It's a cool look. Fake is like really in right now. I wish I had fake everything, too."

"Honey, you better stop now," said Marilyn.

"Sorry, dude—I mean . . . I call real women dude, too. Don't worry. I mean . . . shit. Whatever. I just came in to tell you it's about time to start. Are you about ready?"

"Obviously not, if I look like a fake and a dude. I'll need some more time."

"You look fine. Everybody's starting to get bored looking at each other out there. You look really great, and it's past time to start, so let's get the show on the road." Marilyn turned to Tania, her face turning red through her pale base makeup. Her head quivered tautly, her face contorted into a controlled and frightful mask of graciousness. She said, enunciating each word separately, "Get—out—of—my—dressing—room."

"Dude, *what* is your problem? This is bullshit. This isn't about your ego. This is about Snake. It's time to get out on stage. The show must go on and all that."

"I don't think I need to be listening to *you* about when it's time to leave the dressing room," said Marilyn as she handed Tania a comb. Dreadlocked Tania looked at the comb in her hand for about ten seconds and then threw it back at Marilyn as hard as she could. "Trash!" yelled Marilyn and came at Tania, slamming her into the white tile wall. Tania caught her in the jaw with a right hook that just made her more angry. About this time, Tania remembered that Marilyn was a man—a huge one at that—and that he was coming at her with murder in his eyes. Tania ran to the back wall of the bathroom by the last stall with Marilyn close behind her, but, as Marilyn stopped for a moment to kick off her pumps for the fight, Tania, with her back to the wall, reached into her boot for her locking knife. When she unfolded the blade, Marilyn froze.

"Not my face!" screamed Marilyn, throwing her hands up in front of her face and beginning to whimper. "Don't hurt my face. I'll do anything you say!"

"Shut the fuck up!"

"Please! Please don't hurt my faaace!"

"Just shut up!" cried Tania more in frustration than in anger. "Just get it together, bitch. Just get out on that stage, and I won't cut your face up. Okay?" Marilyn sniffled back her tears, and nodded.

"But I can't go out like this. I'd rather die. You've made me mess up my whole face." In fact, the tears had streaked down the length of her face ruining the whole base coat.

"Five minutes. You have five minutes, and if you're not done, I'm going to come back slicing." Tania slashed the knife through the air with new confidence.

"All right! All right!" When Tania made it out of the bathroom, she leaned against the wall with her eyes wide as she tried to catch hold of her racing thoughts. *Fuck!* she reasoned.

Five minutes later, Marilyn glided out of the bathroom in her fabulous white gown of sequins. Her face looked flawless. She walked out the front door in her pumps, stepped around the bubbling bathtub, and took her place in the floodlights on the landing at the top of the stairs, which would serve as the stage for the evening. All eyes turned toward Marilyn as Tomasso faded the music out from above.

"Ladies and ladies. Many of us knew Snake, and many of us even have examples of this man's art gracing our flesh," said

Marilyn, with a sensual flourish on the word "flesh." "We are here to say good-bye to an artist—a true artist, who thought enough of us to throw this lovely affair and grace us with the unveiling of what he considered his masterpiece, Tania."

Little Marcus looked down on Marilyn from a third story window, hanging on her words, contemplating a short jump and a long sleep. It hurt to look at her, as he remembered the short stretch of happiness he had experienced as her lover. He wished he could explode on impact when he fell and splatter her with blood, like Carrie, and drench everybody else at the party, too. In fact, he wanted to splatter the whole world with blood—wanted the whole world to implode into a neutron star at his point of impact.

"I know many of you would like to say a few words, so why don't I turn the mic over to whoever wants to speak." A very tall, overweight guy with long, blue-black hair walked up the steps. He stepped up to the mic, and Marilyn graciously ceded the floor. The guy's cheap leather jacket fell open, revealing an Exhorter T-shirt.

"Snake did the baddest fuckin' tattoos on the planet," he said bobbing his head and doing a short air guitar performance. "Anything that came up, he could handle it. If a black dude wanted a panther, he could, like, fuckin' do it. If a chick wanted, like, spiritual symbols 'n' shit, he could deal." The guy stopped for a moment, nervously played a little more air guitar, and continued. "A lot of you don't know that he was also a great muscle car mechanic, too. I guess I just want to say," he said, pausing to do an ingenious guitar lick, "I looked up to him. That's it." His friends in the front row applauded and hollered, artists were shaken up, pretty people whispered derisively, and Tomasso snickered. Tania thought it was touching.

"Thank you for sharing," said Marilyn and tossed her hair.

"Who else would like to speak?" A young stick-figure girl with mousy blonde hair walked up and took the mic.

"Snake gave me more than a tattoo. He gave me AIDS. I might not see my twentieth birthday thanks to him. Fuck you, Snake! Rot in hell, Snake! Fuck you all! You're all a bunch of losers!" she said as she threw the mic back at Marilyn. Everyone with a drink drank nervously.

"Well, these things do pop up at funerals," said Marilyn after she regained control of the mic. "But we're here to remember the good things. Um . . . Maybe we should take a break for a while. Tomasso? Let's have some more music." She quickly turned off the mic and disappeared into the school.

"I am not going back out there!" said Marilyn to Tania, who stood inside the door.

Tania opened her palm up and showed Marilyn the folded knife. "Don't fuck with me."

"There are too many witnesses out here. You wouldn't."

Tania unfolded the knife, Marilyn stepped back out to the mic, and the music went off again. She looked around at a bunch of blank faces in the foreground, and farther off, suspended above the courtyard, stood the caged, akimbo figures of the two Catholic schoolgirls with plaid mini skirts. They had stopped dancing.

"I . . . The ceremony has been postponed for a little while," announced Marilyn and walked back inside. The music faded back in. Little Marcus had already gotten one leg out of the window. He retracted it in disgust when he saw her disappear again.

"I just can't do it," said Marilyn to Tania. "The timing's all wrong."

"Dude, we've gotta do it. It's in the will."

Tomasso came bounding down the stairs. "What's going on?" he demanded.

"This dog won't hunt," said Tania cocking her head in Marilyn's direction.

"Marilyn, darling, you looked absolutely scrumptious out there, and everyone is waiting. You ought to know that most of these people came because you are the emcee—they've come to see you, not Tania's tattoo. Don't disappoint your fans. You've handled worse crowds at the Goddess. I know Tania is a little rough around the edges—"

"A little? She's been threatening me with a knife!"

"Tania, did you do that?"

"Only after he slammed me into the wall and backed me into a corner in the bathroom."

"Listen," snapped Tomasso, "this is going nowhere. Now both of you just get back to what you're supposed to be doing."

"Well, who died and made you queen?" asked Marilyn.

"Fuck you!" Tania articulated. Tomasso raised his fist, and would have clocked them both, were it not for the fact that he realized the scene would end up looking like a daytime talk show, and daytime talk shows are not cool. Tomasso lowered his fist, but he had pissed Tania off.

"Try it Tomasso, c'mon!" said Tania, flipping the knife open. Since she bought the knife a year and a half before, it had never been unfolded, but tonight she had flipped it open three times, and she was starting to like the feeling of power. "C'mon." Tomasso decided he should disarm her and confidently lunged for her wrist. His speed didn't do the trick this time, as Tania reflexively slashed with the knife, cutting him between the middle and fourth finger of his right hand. Tomasso stepped back, and a rivulet of blood trickled down his forearm.

"Oh, my God," said Tania dropping the knife. "I'm sorry. I'm sorry dude. Are you okay? Let me see. Let me look at it."

She held her hands with her finger tips spread and trembling before her mouth.

"Stay away!" shouted Tomasso, examining the wound. He could see it was minor—a three-stitch job—but Tania realized she was backing away and hitting herself in the head again. A few guests had seen the whole thing, and headed for the door. Before long, they would spread the word that the party had ended. Tania had to do something, so she went out before the mic, which screeched feedback when she turned it on. "This on?" She looked around, and realized she had never had that many people staring at her at the same time before.

She had often found herself the center of attention, but now several hundred people stared at her—not amorously, not depreciatingly, but waiting to hear what she had to say. Most of the time, she could barely get one person to listen to what she had to say. But there they all stood, looking at her and waiting for her words. Surrounded on three sides by hundreds of people, Tania had never felt so alone, but she calmed herself by looking at the mic. "Okay, so Snake was no angel," she began. "He may be dead now, but when he was alive, he was more alive than a lot of us. I mean, that girl has a right to hate him, but maybe she would never have been as alive as she was with that tattoo she got, whatever it was, and I wonder what they'll be saying about her when she goes, or about any of us when we go.

"Like, it seems like our lives are so fucking empty and like in a dark corner, you know? But Snake was always burning up with, like, passion and just always so, like, fully into what he was doing, and if you got one of his tattoos it's like you got some of the light from the fire, you know? I mean, there's a million ways to die young around here, and a red carpet out in front of all of 'em. You all have friends that died on you, and you can usually blame them for it, easy, or blame somebody else for it, or blame yourself, and you'd be right either way, but they're still dead. I know a bunch of you, and nobody here's an angel as far as I can see. I just cut my friend's hand like an idiot, and I'm really sorry about it. Worse than that, I think I really fucked my boyfriend over, and he's really the coolest dude I've ever known, and I know I'm a mess and don't deserve him.

"I know Snake was really sorry about being an asshole, too, 'cause I got to know him pretty good when he was finishing my tat. So, look. Snake played rough with, like, the universe, and he probably stands for, like, everything we hate about ourselves, and also the like cosmic energy we love about ourselves. So, just, like, think of him as family, okay? He was one of our tribe, so just give him his props. He decorated us good, and that should mean something. I know you came here for a party, but I had to say what was on my mind."

Just then, Marilyn stepped out onto the landing and asked for the mic back. Tania gave it to her. "Tania's right. We're not saints, but we all have a shining inner being that glitters if you just throw some light on it, and Snake did, too." Little Marcus got his stubby leg out of the window again, and began to draw the other one up. "I have been an absolute bitch, myself, and I have an awful confession to make," Marilyn continued, "and I need to apologize to each and every one of my fans." Little Marcus sat with both feet hanging into space. "For as long as you've known me, I've just been Marilyn the drag queen, and that's the way a very special man knew me—loved me, and I walked away from him. He wanted me to marry him, and get a domestic partnership. But I told him my lies, too—many awful lies. Marcus, if you're out in the crowd, I need to tell you that—Marcus, I do love you but I'm a woman. I'm not a transvestite. I'm a real woman who is pregnant with your child, and I'd still marry you if you'd have me, though I know that would probably be impossible for you."

Little Marcus froze, his mind reeling from all the thoughts crowding his big head. He thought of how particular Marilyn had been in bed, and how she never let him touch her down there with his hands. *It could be true. Oh, fuck me! It is true!* Little Marcus sat, stunned, with his legs dangling in mid-air. He remained oblivious to the spectacle that then ensued in the playground three stories below. But as his field of vision went dark, just as he fainted, he did register the distinct sensation of falling from a great height.

chapter 19.
GATE CRASHERS

THE SAME CITY WHICH MARCUS ONE MINUTE BEFORE HAD celebrated leaving, now seemed like his only escape. Before him, the interstate stretched like a long gauntlet, but to his right, over the railing, stretched a seemingly endless warren of old wooden houses and chaotic rooftops. On those streets below, he could lose the cops. On the interstate, he would be caught quickly. He could not possibly make it out of town now, so he decided to take the only reasonable course of action (barring surrender) and took the next exit down into the welcoming confusion of New Orleans's Treme, Faubourg Marigny, and Bywater sections. As the Roadrunner glided down the interstate exit ramp, descending past rooftop-level, the enraged police car squawked orders from the rear. *I can lose them*, thought Marcus. He had revised his plan. It no longer included Snake, except in as much as Marcus planned to ditch him. Marcus now planned to escape on foot at the first possible opportunity. Snake's sister could have laid Snake out under sun-flooded stained glass windows and a giant, full-color, bleeding Christ on the cross, with pipe organs blaring and scripture flying, for all Marcus cared at that point.

The Roadrunner ran the red light at the corner of oak-lined Esplanade Avenue. Marcus floored it. A couple of blocks later, he took a right into a rundown neighborhood, with the cops still on his tail, though now not as close as they had been. He ran over a cat as he floored it to the end of another block, and he almost struck a little black kid. "Bugger!" shouted Marcus as he began to lose heart for the chase, but when the siren drew near again, his reason flew out the window again. Behind him, the mother of the child ran across the road to grab her child, screaming "My baby! My baby!" The police car slammed on the breaks to keep from hitting her. It lost control and hit a parked Impala hard. Marcus felt like he had something lodged in his windpipe as he considered the narrowly averted consequences of his recklessness, but took advantage of the wreck to gun the car again. He took an aimless and circuitous path through the endless neighborhoods of shotgun homes.

Periodically he could hear sirens, sometimes nearer and sometimes farther, but he needed to get free of them to escape on foot in an area where he wouldn't look completely out of place. As a precaution against getting identified by anyone, he ripped open the package of pantyhose he had bought, and pulled them down over his face. The legs of the hose hung at the sides of his head like farcical ears, and, as he looked in the mirror, he vowed to remember to get stockings next time. He looked like a depressed rabbit, with his nose all flattened out as the printed finger on Snake's "I'M WITH STUPID" T-shirt pointed at him accusingly.

Soon, the sirens no longer sounded, and he figured he had lost them. Looking at the street sign at a corner, he realized he didn't have the slightest idea where he was, but a police car jumped in front of him at the intersection as its siren flipped on, screaming and flashing. The cop in the front leaned out of the window with a shotgun, and Marcus just managed to duck before a blast slammed a large hole in the Roadrunner's windshield and turned the rest of the shatterproof glass into an intricate spider web of fractures. Looking out the rear window, past the high, reenforced headrest, Marcus threw her in reverse, and stepped on it as tires screeched. But he couldn't keep the car under control. He hit a parked Lincoln. "Bollocks!" He kicked out what was left of his windshield, and saw the police car's headlights appearing through the cloud of noxious rubber smoke he had just kicked up for them. The cop on the passenger side had begun to lean out the window with the shotgun again. Marcus threw the car into first and drove straight at them. The cop with the shotgun quickly disappeared into the cruiser again like a turtle's head. The Roadrunner smashed into the police car at about fifteen miles per hour—enough to disorient them—not enough to damage their engines.

This time, Marcus backed up more cautiously, made it to the corner, and then crossed the street, where he put the car in first again and tried to turn left onto the street he had just crossed. As he did so, the police car came careening out, attempting to block his escape, but slammed into the right passenger door. Snake toppled over on Marcus's lap. Marcus got the car moving again, but another police car had come up behind him. Slowly he realized that he had drawn near the end of the chase, as he stepped on the gas again and tore off down the street followed now by two police cars. Another police car pulled out at a cross street he had just passed. Almost had him blocked in. "Bugger all!" He had dusted them in the straightaways, but now many cars would soon converge on the whole area. Marcus would find himself trapped—probably executed on the spot, even though he had just left three police cars blocks behind.

Yet something looked familiar about the block that he was now passing. He slowed down with a screech, and recognized the iron fence of Julie's school. As he drew nearer, he saw the crowds of people in the playground. Without a thought, he drove up over the curb to the gate and stopped there. He gunned the engine, and made a frightful racket. The guests cleared a wide path. Marcus looked up and saw Tania, standing next to Marilyn at the top of the steps. From across the playground, their eyes met. Marcus drove the Roadrunner into the middle of the playground, got out of the car leaving the motor running, and pulled Snake into the driver's seat.

Police cars screeched to a halt out front, and Tania cried into the mic to "Lock the gate! Lock the gate!" Two young punk rock girls slammed the gates shut and clasped down the padlock just as two cops came running up.

"Open the fuckin' gate, you fuckin' bitch!" said a tall cop with a protruding gut.

"I don't know the combination. Sorry," said the girl with the bleached chemotherapy haircut. The other girl, purple streaks in her blue-black hair, tilted her head to the side, squinted her eyes, and stuck out just the tip of her tongue at the cop.

With some difficulty, Marcus managed to get Snake's hands placed on the steering wheel. With this accomplished, he pulled out his gallon jug of gasoline, poured a large amount on the five-gallon jug, the seat, and Snake, and laid down a long trail of gasoline away from the car. "Get away from the car!" Tania shouted into the mic.

Women began to scream, and the crowd drew away from the car in a large circle of panic. They packed themselves against the walls of the school and madly climbed and tumbled into the windows. Four more police cars pulled up out front, sirens screaming, lights flashing wildly. The occupants jumped out bristling with firearms. Tomasso, looking down from his window above the front steps, recognized the morose rabbit as Big Marcus and began to giggle.

Marcus was ready to set the car ablaze, but he had forgotten something: he didn't have a light. He saw two cops climbing the fence of the playground about twenty feet away. In despair, he prepared to run from the cops in defeat, but he heard Tania's voice from the loudspeakers. "Dude!" He looked up and saw Tania at the top of the stairs, equidistant with the cops in the opposite direction. She waved something in her hand, then threw, and he saw the perfect arching trajectory of a disposable lighter careening toward him. He caught it, and reflexively struck it on the gasoline trail. The blue flame seemed to glide in slow motion toward the Roadrunner where Snake sat behind the wheel.

When the flash of the explosion appeared, Marcus could have sworn everything went silent—he heard neither the sirens, the screaming guests, the music, nor the curses of the cops who could not get through the gate. The fireball expanded and drove skyward with a seemingly interminable progress. Tania thrilled to the sight of it, but let out an abbreviated yelp as she saw the dwarf topple from the third-story window. Marilyn, also seemingly in slow motion, screamed "Marcus!" and stood transfixed.

When Tomasso saw the fireball go up, he started laughing uncontrollably. He popped a CD into the player, and, with one earphone pressed up to his left ear, pressed the start button with a thumb jutting from a bloody T-shirt wrapped around his lacerated hand. He pushed the volume slider to the highest volume he could pump into the speakers without distortion. Nobody had heard the record before. Muted, synthetic beats and sublime chord changes scintillated in an oceanic background of complex reverb, and a powerful, saw-toothed sequencer riff shifted phase during its course and almost seemed to speak. The music was eyelidless beauty and violence, burning all emotion with robotic flame-throwers of desire, until all that remained was an ash of elation.

Big Marcus, unaware of the Little Marcus tragedy, looked at the silent fireball, and felt the music razoring through his being as part of the silence. He laughed, felt the tears streaming down his cheeks, felt the sensation of arm hair singeing, and the not so pleasurable sensation of his panty hose melting. However, the charm soon broke, and all the sound burst in upon his consciousness again. The melancholy hare bounded up the steps and grabbed Tania.

"We have to get out of here!"

"But Little Marcus! He fell!"

"There's no time! We have to run!"

"No! Wait!" Tania turned toward the Roadrunner. The flames still boiled out of the muscle-car, and she felt the skin tighten on her cheeks as she faced the radiant heat from her vantage point at the top of the steps. She caught momentary glimpses of police through the flames, rubber-smoke, and rippling heat distortion. Cops stalked around outside, checked by the conflagration. They could neither enter the playground through the arching iron gate or scale the eight-foot, turn-of-the-century fence with its lance-tipped bars.

Tania tossed her head forward and tied her thick dreads up on her head by wrapping one of them around the rest. When she stood back up, the dreads stood out and made her look like a palm tree. "Okay. It's time. Here it is!" Tania said into the mic, and her voice immediately focused the crowd of hipsters that now shrank back from the blaze in a wide circle. Despite the initial panicked shrieks when the fireball had gone up, most of the guests still held their cocktails. Hundreds of wide eyes looked up at her. The faces of the hitherto cool now wore the rapt expressions of children when you tell them a good story.

Tania lightly held both ends of her silky, black shawl in her fingers, raised her arms until they reached straight out, and turned her back to the crowd. Then she dropped the shawl from her shoulders. Her backless gown let the snake tattoo finally show its entire writhing length, from its head on her right hand, all the way across her shoulders, to the slithering tail on her left hand. She closed her eyes. At first, she could only hear the roar of the flames, but another roar joined and soon overpowered it as the jaded crowd let out a collective shout of approval long repressed for want of anything cool enough to cheer for. She threw her head back and opened her eyes on the amber, mercury-vapor-lit sky. Marcus thought he saw the corner of her eye glisten, as if a tear were forming. It could have been the heat or the smoke, he reasoned, *but isn't it always?*

The police now stopped their pacing outside and looked on, an azure grove beyond the fence. Something in the blaring dance track seemed to hold the world in check, and the cops seemed transfixed more by the power and the volume of the music than by the heat. Tomasso had thought to wait until he had gotten signed to let anyone hear the alien trance music he had been laboring so long to record in secrecy, but the time had obviously come.

The crowd, which had packed itself tightly against the building, had broken Little Marcus's fall. He knocked an artist unconscious and broke the collar bone of a drug dealer as he landed, but Little Marcus survived unscathed except for a few broken ribs. Now he lay on the ground looking at the low amber sky. As the music flowed through his mind, he remembered Marilyn's revelation and laughed, even though his broken ribs made the act torture. Later, the paramedics were able to get his laughter under control with a Valium injection, but he still giggled deliriously. They would ask him if he knew his name and the date, to which he would laugh again. Between his desperate gasps for breath they would hear him say, "I'm a fucking breeder!"

Somehow, regardless of the sirens, flames, and chaos, the crowd danced and generally had a great time. Big Marcus looked on from behind Tania, and realized his moment of thoughtless action lay behind him. He had held the fire but his fate, he knew, was to never be consumed by it. Though he had really let go for a moment, as he drove the speeding chunk of metal, he had now slipped out of that moment of oneness with action that spelled his momentary release from his prison of self-awareness. But now he no longer felt alone. They were three. Marcus had become the audience again, Tania had become the art, and Snake was the fire.

The kid with the jester's hat walked up the steps, grabbed the mic, stared at the burning Roadrunner, and said, with a supremely spaced-out inflection, "Snake is *toast*, man."

chapter 20.
SMACK

Marcus and Tania beat it back to the apartment fully expecting to get caught at any moment, so they did the only sensible thing; they made love all night, and Tania actually managed to have an orgasm without any restraints. Just before dawn, Marcus made tea and went out on the gallery. He nervously eyed Decatur Street as if he expected police cars to pull up in front at any moment. As he sat at his little table, he noticed that some extremely energetic and resourceful bug had figured out how to get around the screen and immolate himself inside Marcus's hanging light fixture. Marcus raised his glass of tea in a silent toast.

After the sun rose and the restaurant workers began to hose down the sidewalks like any other day, Marcus went back inside. He sat down on the bed, and turned on the television that sat on the bedside table. The early report began, and a beautiful black woman in a red blazer with shoulder pads began to read the headlines.

"Last night, a party in honor of a deceased tattoo artist at an abandoned Ninth Ward school turned to chaos as a high-speed chase ended in flames right in the middle of the celebration." Footage of fire fighters attacking the smoldering Roadrunner with fire extinguishers then flashed on the screen. "In a bizarre twist of events, the burning car actually

175

contained the dead body of the tattoo artist known as Snake. Police say his sister alerted them to the theft of the car containing the body, but would not say what the body was doing in the car." Then a sweaty older detective with his hair neatly combed back came on the screen and began to speak. "When, uh, the stolen vehicle turned into the grounds and the perpetrator, uh, ignited it, we were, uh, unable to, uh, pursue because of the, uh, intense heat and flames. We're questioning a lot of witnesses, and we're confident that, uh, we're gonna catch the guy." Then some wide shots of the school and the street came on while the anchor continued. "Neighbors and some eyewitnesses suggested that the burning of the car may have been a cult-related ritual." A thin woman with a baby in her arms flashed on the screen and said, "Dat was some kind of voodoo ovuh day, baby. Dey had a gir' in a black dress wid a snake tattoo dancin' when dat man was boinin' up. Like ta make me sick!" The anchor spoke again. "We'll keep you up to date on this bizarre story as details become available. In other news, the president—" Marcus clicked the TV off. *Bollocks. We're stars. They're bound to pull out the stops, now.* He lay down on the bed and put his arms around Tania, who lay facing the other way. She sighed and roused herself a little.

"I love you," said Marcus, sure that their days were numbered. Tania smiled, and went to take her bath.

☉☉☉

The cops never identified them. It could have been an actual miracle. Nobody at the party would tell the police anything, and, after a week, Marcus began to relax. Eventually a couple of bored-looking cops showed up at the Goddess to question Tania, who denied being present at the affair. The free drinks and the big smile she gave them, in addition to

the fact that there was a detail cop working the door, probably got them to drop the subject. She questioned them
attentively about the incident, remarking how she needed to
know if there was someone else in town with dreadlocks
and a snake tattoo, so she could be prepared for further mis-
understandings. But Tania didn't even break a sweat. When
she was behind the bar, she felt invincible.

Tania and Marcus fell into a domestic rhythm almost
immediately. Eventually, Munchy began to allow Marcus near
him, and even take him for walks and vice-versa. Marcus
began to work again translating, and the money began to
come back in. For perhaps the first time in his life, he stayed
happy for days on end. After about two weeks, however,
Tania lost the glow of infatuation and began looking for the
door. She got her car fixed, planned her escape, and one day
just drove off. Marcus found a note:

Dear Marcus,
By the time you read this, I will be gone. I'm going to California.
Don't wait on a call, because I'm not going to call you. But if you're
wondering, I didn't leave because of anything you did. I want you
to know I think you are really cool, and you'll find some chick who
will treat you right, but it is not me. This kind of shit always hap-
pens with me. I just like to be free. I will always remember the things
you did for me, and I know I owe you, but I can't pay you back.
Sorry. I have never been in love but if I could just decide to fall in
love with somebody, it would be you. I really felt like maybe I loved
you for a while there but it went away like usual. Maybe we will
run into each other again someday. I know this is going to hurt you.
I'm not being stuck up I just know that you have sensitive feelings
and that's good. I am kind of jealous of that. But really you shouldn't
be wasting your time on me. You can do better. Promise.
Sincerely, Tania

☺☺☺

Tomasso could only find heroin in response to Marcus's desperate phone call. Marcus sat at the table, with Tomasso, melting some brown into a few drops of water in a spoon. Tomasso held the disposable lighter under the tablespoon, and Marcus held the spoon and stirred the liquid with the tip of the disposable syringe. They didn't talk. Tomasso's face looked somber and bony. Marcus palmed the needle and drew the liquid into the syringe by hooking his thumbnail under the end of the plunger and pulling back while holding the spoon. When the shot was ready, he held it out to Tomasso. Tomasso yanked back his belt, tightening it around his arm, wrapping it under, and clenching it between his teeth. Marcus thought this was a little strange, because Tomasso's veins normally bulged even without the belt. This was going to be like shooting fish in a barrel, he thought. Tomasso registered immediately, and Marcus watched his blood mix with the liquid in the syringe. Then Tomasso pushed the plunger all the way in and let go of the belt. It was a lot. Tomasso's eyes narrowed, and Marcus could only see the whites. His head teetered like a stack of dishes. Marcus prepared another spoonful and drew it into the other needle a few c.c.'s more than what Tomasso had gotten. He had less luck. His veins were small and deep, and he had to stick himself seven times before he registered. Then he pushed, too, and disappeared into a silence.

When he finally opened his eyelids an eighth of an inch, he noticed Tomasso was not there anymore. Marcus managed to get up and walk into the bathroom, where he knelt in front of the toilet, and it seemed to him as if clouds rolled in the window over him. He felt the vomit coming up, but didn't care. There wasn't much in there, anyway. He got up and washed his face. Then he got into the empty bathtub and lay there, his awareness swimming in a sea of vivid images of many of his old friends, some of them deceased. He felt as if he were floating in the current of a holy river seeing them so clearly, especially the dead ones, everyone smiling in the portraits that floated into his retinal circus—portraits of everyone at their best, and there was Tania, too—the toothy smile, the heavy dreads, the glittering eyes, legs crossed sitting on a barstool in the velvet darkness of some 2:00 A.M. bar—the smile generous, the eyes delighted, and Marcus knew he was fucked for a long time, but the images kept coming, and he welcomed them freely because he was on too much smack to feel any pain, and he smiled, a little, and thought *This is the way it has always been. Alone with my pictures.*

👁👁👁

Tania drove through the Texas night, calming her nerves with cigarettes, a habit she had not yet fully acquired. Here, on the road, all of her thoughts seemed like lost letters addressed to Marcus, or phone calls dialed to Marcus's number, but she had lost the knack of hurting. Thinking of him was just a habit. The hurting would never be strong enough to counter the wanting. The circuit was burnt out. She sucked hard on the Marlboro red, and the empty rolling country came up in front of her and slipped away behind her in the moonlight. Munchy's well-groomed head lay across her leg. Now she was not exactly thinking, and in the void of thought, the past, present, and future and the cities she had lived in all merged into one giant now-city that never sleeps, and she knew somehow that Marcus was still with her, and Snake was still with her, and so was Jimmy, and her love was just too big to focus, ever.

AUTHOR'S FINAL NOTE

WHEN I WAS DOING THE INTERVIEWS WITH TANIA FOR THIS BOOK, she was back in town again, and we kind of developed a little sexual relationship. She felt terribly guilty about it, even though she was no longer seeing Marcus. (I guess seeing what happened to him sort of gave her a shock, but he's a lot better now.) When Marcus finally found out about us, she said she couldn't stand herself and was not going to see me, and refused to speak to me any more. Last time I heard, she was working for a record company in Hollywood, but I have an idea she has moved on by now. Marcus will not speak to me, either, though I feel, now, that in telling his story, I was telling my own story as well. I dealt with losing her the same way he did, and I still miss her terribly, but I think my sense of humor saved me, and it has also gotten me out of that damned city.

With so many transplanted people living in and around the French Quarter, all of them bent on imagining the place to their own specifications, you can take one wrong step and find yourself tumbling into a total void, as if the cement, iron, and bricks themselves have been dreamed by so many people that they are evaporating into an imaginary metropolis that is not all that carefully mortared together. And somehow the people who get assimilated into New Orleans also seem to simultaneously lose substance and gain significance as they transpose themselves into the dream of the place. Now I wonder if I really feel this identification with Marcus. Did he really exist at all, as such, or was he some two-dimensional figment of his own imagination or mine? Did I know him at all, or did I just project my own personality onto him? And I have to wonder if I really miss Tania as much as I do. But I'm sure I will end up in New Orleans again someday, and all of these people I have accused of being mirages will have beating hearts again and their own smiles and smells and ways, independent of my memories of them, and they will see me and have that strange experience of seeing someone alive who they assumed was dead and nothing will be the way it was.

BORN IN NEW ORLEANS IN 1962, REX ROSE has led an unconventional life. His father withdrew him from the third grade for ideological reasons, and he never returned to school steadily until entering Tulane University. In the intervening years, he played electric guitar for bands, worked in a Bourbon Street sex toy shop, shucked oysters for seven years at a New Orleans bar, and traveled extensively in Mexico. After Rose began his studies at Tulane, he wrote a monthly technology column for *Tribe* Magazine and was one of the magazine's journeymen music critics. He earned a BA in English at Tulane University on the John Kennedy Toole Writing Scholarship, studied law for a year at LSU Law School, and eventually entered the LSU Creative Writing program, where he earned his Master of Fine Arts in creative writing under Andrei Codrescu, Vance Bourjaily, Moira Crone, Jim Bennett, and Mark Poirier. Rex Rose is a contributing editor for *Exquisite Corpse* at http://exquisitecorpse.org. *Toast* is his first novel.